W9-AQC-482

The Consolation of Nature

The

CONSOLATION

of

NATURE

and Other Stories

VALERIE MARTIN

Boston

HOUGHTON MIFFLIN COMPANY

1 9 8 8

Library of Congress Cataloging-in-Publication Data

Martin, Valerie.
The consolation of nature and other stories.

I. Title.
PS3563.A7295C66   1988   813'.54   87-19735
ISBN 0-395-46788-8

PRINTED IN THE UNITED STATES OF AMERICA

S 10 9 8 7 6 5 4 3 2 1

"The Consolation of Nature" first appeared in the *New Orleans Review* (Volume 9, Number 2, Fall 1982). "Sea Lovers" first appeared in the *Black Warrior Review* (Volume 11, Number 2, Spring 1985).

for my daughter, Adrienne

"Come hither, Son," I heard Death say;
"I did not will a grave
Should end thy pilgrimage to-day,
But I, too, am a slave!"

– From "The Subalterns"
THOMAS HARDY

Contents

The Consolation of Nature

to Chris Wiltz

LILY'S HAIR was her mother's pride. In the afternoons, when she came home from school, she sat at the kitchen table, her head resting on the back of her chair, while her mother dragged the wooden brush through the long strands. Lily told her mother what had happened at school that day, or she talked of her many ambitions. Her mother, preoccupied with her work, holding up a thick lock and pulling out with her fingers a particularly tenacious knot, responded laconically. She looked upon this ritual of her daughter's hair as a solemn duty, like the duties of feeding and clothing.

One afternoon they sat so engaged, conversing softly while outside the rain beat against the house. Lily's mother observed that she couldn't take much more rain, that it would surely rot her small, carefully tended vegetable garden, that it seemed to be rotting her own imagination. Lily agreed. It had rained steadily for three days. Her head rose and fell, like a flower on its stalk, with each stroke of her mother's care, and each time it did she lifted her eyes a bit, taking in a larger section of the tiled floor before her.

Her mother shouted and threw the brush toward the stove.

Lily sat up and looked after the brush. She was quick enough to see the disappearing tail and hindquarters of a rat as he scurried beneath the refrigerator. These parts, Lily thought, were unusually large, and this notion was quickly confirmed by her mother's cry as she clung momentarily to the edge of the table. "Good Christ," her mother said. "That's the biggest rat I've ever seen."

Lily drew her legs up under her and watched the spot where the rat had been. Her mother was already on the telephone to her father's secretary. "No," she said, "don't bother him. Just tell him there's a rat as big as a cat in the kitchen and he needs to stop at the K & B on the way home for a trap. Tell him to get the biggest trap they make." When she got off the phone, she suggested that they move to the dining room to finish Lily's hair. "It's the rain," her mother said as she closed the kitchen door carefully behind them. "The river is so high it's driving them out."

Lily sat at the dining table and pulled her long hair up over the back of her chair. Her mother resumed her vigorous brushing. It was strange, Lily thought, to sit at the big dining table in the dull afternoon light. The steady beating of the rain against the windows made her drowsy and her mind wandered. She thought of how the river must look, swollen with brown water, swirling along hurriedly toward the Gulf of Mexico. She had never been to the mouth of the river, though she had gone down as far as Barataria once with her father. It had not been, as she had imagined, a neat little breaking-up of water fingers, the way it looked on the map. Instead, it was a great marsh with a road through it. There were fishing shacks on piers, wood, and other odd debris scattered in the shallow areas. She remembered that trip clearly, though two years had passed and she had been, she thought, only nine at the time. They had stopped to buy shrimp and her father had laughed at her impatience to have hers peeled. That was when she had learned to peel shrimp, and she did it so well that the job now regularly fell to her.

Her mother had not stopped thinking of the rat. "I can't get over his coming out in broad daylight like that," she remarked as she pulled the loose hairs from the brush.

"Who?" Lily asked.

"That rat," her mother replied. "I don't even want to cook dinner with that thing in there."

Lily could think of no response, so she stood up, turning to her mother and fluffing her hair out past her shoulders.

"That looks lovely," her mother said, touching Lily's hair at the temple. Then, as if she were shy of her daughter's beauty, she drew her hand away. "Do you have a lot of homework?" she asked.

"Plenty," Lily said. "I guess I'd better get to it."

When her father arrived that evening at his usual time, it was with chagrin that his wife and daughter learned he hadn't gotten their message and had come home trapless to his family.

"Well, go out and get one now," her mother complained. "I don't want to spend a night in the house with that thing alive."

"It's pouring down rain," Lily's father protested. "I'll get one tomorrow. He's probably moved on already anyway."

"Give me the keys," she said. "I'll get it myself."

Lily stood in the kitchen doorway during this argument and she stepped aside as her mother came storming past her, the keys clutched in her angry fist. Her father sat down at the kitchen table and smiled after his affronted mate.

"Did you see this giant rat?" he asked Lily.

"Sort of," she said.

"Are you sure he wasn't a mouse?"

"I think it was a rat," Lily speculated. "His back was kind of high, not flat like a mouse."

"When have you ever seen a rat?" her father asked impatiently.

Lily looked away. She had, she realized, never seen a rat, except in pictures, and she knew that if she said "In pictures," her father would consider her to have less authority than she had already. "He was big, Dad," she said at last, turning away.

When her mother pulled the trap from its purple bag, Lily felt a twinge of sympathy for the rat. The board was large, the bar, which snapped closed when it was set, was wide enough to accommodate Lily's hand, the spring was devilishly strong and so tight that her father forced the bar back with difficulty. He tested it with a wooden spoon, and the bar snapped closed, lifting the board well off the floor. Her father baited it with a slice of potato, and the family turned out the lights and settled in their beds. Lily lay with her eyes open, listening for the snap of the bar, but she didn't hear it, and while she was listening she fell asleep.

The next morning the trap was discovered just as it had been left. Lily's father gave her mother a cold skeptical look and sprung the trap again with a spoon. Her mother concentrated on cooking the breakfast, allowing the matter to drop. When he was gone to work she turned to Lily as if to a conspirator and said, "I'll get some poison today and we can try again tonight."

Lily didn't think of the rat again during the day. Her school work was oppressive, but at lunch break, for the first time that week, the students were turned out of doors. The clouds had cleared off, leaving a sky of hectic blue, a sun that beat down on the wet ground with the thoroughness of a shower. Lily and her best friend sat on the breezeway, watching the braver students, who sloshed through the puddles in search of exercise. They discussed their summer plans and confided in each other their mutual fear that they would be separated the following fall.

"If I get that grouch Miss Bambula," Lily's friend said, "I think I'll die. She looks just like a horse."

Lily wondered which would be worse, to be with her friend and have Miss Bambula or to be without her friend and Miss Bambula. One of the boys in the yard hailed the two girls, holding up for their long-distance inspection the squirming green body of a lizard. Lily stood up and went out to him, for she liked lizards, and this one, she saw at once, was of a good size.

That afternoon, when her mother brushed her hair, the rat didn't appear. "Maybe your father's right," her mother said hopefully. Later, after she had practiced piano, Lily rejoined her mother in the kitchen to help with dinner. She sat at the table with a large bowl of green beans, which she proceeded to snap, throwing the ends into a small bowl, the fat centers into another. Her mother stood at the counter, peeling potatoes. They worked without speaking and it was so quiet in the room that they heard the scratching of the rat's claws against the floor before they saw him. They both turned, looking in shocked silence at the refrigerator. His ugly face appeared first; then he took a few timid steps forward and stood before them. Lily saw that his black lips were drawn back over his teeth and his cheeks pulsated with his nervous breathing. She sucked in her own breath and dropped the bean she was holding. The rat made a sudden dash for the stove, moving so quickly that Lily's mother let out a little cry as she jumped out of his path. "Mama," Lily said softly as they both bolted for the kitchen door. Her mother held the swinging door open and wrapped her arm protectively around her daughter's shoulder as she passed through. In the dining room they stood together and Lily allowed herself, for a moment, the luxury of closing her eyes against her mother's shoulder. "Don't worry, baby," her mother said. "I got the poison this morning; we'll get him tonight."

Lily's father was incredulous when they told him of the intruder's boldness and he smiled in disbelief when Lily, holding up her hands, estimated the creature's true dimensions. "She's not kidding," her mother said angrily. "He's really big. We got a good look at him this time."

"All right," her father said. "We'll put out the trap again. I just wish he'd show his face when I'm here."

"Christ," her mother replied. "That's not my fault. If he's still here tomorrow I'll take his picture. Would you believe that?"

"That's not a bad idea," her father said.

That night, before they went to bed, the family gathered in the kitchen and laid out their arsenal. The trap was baited and placed near the wall; the poison, which was inside a plastic box with a hole at one end, was placed near the stove with the hole turned toward the wall.

"Can he get in that little hole?" Lily asked.

"I hope so," her mother replied.

Alone in her bed, Lily slept, then woke, then slept again. Toward morning she opened her eyes abruptly, with the sensation that she had cause to do so. She raised herself on one elbow and looked out into the darkness of her room. She could see nothing, but she heard distinctly a scratching sound, the sound, she knew at once, of claws against wood. She fell back and put her hands over her mouth, as if to hold in a scream, though she made no sound. Her heart pounded so furiously that she could hear it, and she felt in her legs, which were drawn up now beneath the sheet, the sudden ebbing of strength that usually follows a nightmare. The sound continued and it seemed to her that it became louder, closer, as the moments passed. She consoled herself with the thought that the rat would doubtless find little to interest him in her room and would soon opt for the swift or slow death that awaited him in the kitchen. If only she'd put a trap in her room, she thought.

The scratching was very close and then, when it sounded as though the creature was under the bed, abruptly it stopped. Lily breathed uneasily, afraid and unable to move. Then she heard a sound she was never to forget, the metallic protest of the bed springs as they received the weight of the animal's body. Lily's eyes burned into the humid dark air and she opened her mouth, but still no sound came. She had begun to perspire; her gown clung wetly to her narrow chest. Again she heard the squeaking springs and this time she knew exactly where the sound came from. The rat was just behind her head and though she couldn't see him and didn't have the strength even to turn her head so that she might see him, she felt the nervous twitching of his snout, the horrible inhalation of his breath, as he pulled himself up over the headboard of the bed and looked down upon the paralyzed young girl before him.

For a moment the animal contemplated her, and then, as if they were one, both moved. The rat sprang forward, his front legs stretching out before him as his back feet propelled him out into the air. Lily, finding her strength and her voice at once, sat up, throwing her hands over her head and screaming "No!" But it was too late. Her left hand encountered the rat's side and inadvertently she slapped him toward her own back. He landed squarely on the top of her head, and as she swung her legs over the side of the bed and rose to her feet, he slid down her back. His body was enormously heavy and in his panic he clawed at her hair, tangling himself and enraging Lily so that she threw herself against the wall, thinking to crush him. This gave him the leverage he needed to pull free of her hair. He slipped down over her buttocks and dropped to the floor. He was running when he hit the wood, scrambling back toward the bed. Lily was already in the hall. Now, she thought, she could run until she dropped. But she only ran to her parents' door, throwing it open before her with a scream. Her mother was raised up on her elbow looking at her; her father sat on the edge of the bed fumbling for his slippers. It was to her father that she ran, but not for comfort. She caught him by his shoulders, forcing him to fall back across the sheets, and she held him down there, her hair falling wildly about her as she screamed into his astonished face, "You kill him, you kill him now! Go and kill him now!"

Her mother sat up, pulling back Lily's hair, feeling her neck and shoulders frantically. "Did he bite you?" she asked. "Are you cut?" Then Lily turned on her mother, thinking that she would strike her, but when she was folded into the eager, smothering embrace, she gave in and clung to her mother's neck, hugging her close. Her mother glared over the girl's shoulders at the still prostrate form of her husband and repeated to him the injunction his daughter had just given him. "Go and kill him now," she said. "Don't leave this house until that animal is dead."

Lily's father sat up and resumed fumbling for his slippers.

Lily and her mother lay locked together and neither watched him as he shuffled off toward the bathroom. They clung to each other, pulling the sheets up and adjusting the pillows so that they could sleep as they had when Lily was a baby, with their arms around each other. Outside, the rain began, softly at first, punctuated with the low rumble of thunder and flashes of heat lightning that radiated like nerves across the sky. Lily's father had turned on the light in the hall and she could hear him in the kitchen, opening the refrigerator, running water in the sink. The rain grew more intense; it beat insistently against the window in her parents' room and she thought of how it must be outdoors, beating the flowers down into the already water-logged soil, beating the leaves back on the trees. She thought especially of the big plantain tree in the side yard, of how it bent down in the rain, its great leaves shiny and smooth, like sheets of brilliantly painted plastic. The rain washed over the house and seemed to carry great waves of sleep with it, impossible to resist.

In the morning Lily and her mother found her father asleep at the kitchen table, his arms spread out before him, his cheek pressed against the wood, his mouth slack from weariness. He had prepared himself a cup of coffee, which sat on the table near his left hand, but he had not drunk half of it.

Lily's mother woke him impatiently. He lifted his head, rubbed his eyes, and looked sleepily at his wife, then at his daughter. He put out his hand to Lily and drew her toward him. "Are you OK now, baby?" he said. "Are you sure it wasn't a dream?" Then, as she was about to protest, his face changed. He looked across her shoulder and Lily knew, without turning, what he saw. Her mother followed his gaze and changed her expression from aggravation to horror. Lily turned around and saw him. He had come out silently and stood, calm, though as he was always, poised for flight. He moved his ugly head back and forth, watching, sniffing, and Lily could hear again the horrible sound of his breathing. He confronted them and they couldn't look away, for his boldness was as wonderful as his size. Lily's mother reached back suddenly, took the half-full coffee cup, and threw it with all her strength at the animal. He was gone before the cup hit the ground.

For two days and nights the rat was under siege. The animal sensed the change in his situation and responded with the obsessive wiles of the hunted. Traps and poison failed to entice him, though he made frequent appearances in the vicinity of both. The family spent the weekend in an ecstasy of determination, baiting all possible hiding places with poison. Lily's parents moved the stove and refrigerator out from the wall. Lily herself helped to seal off any holes they discovered, along the baseboards, in the window casings, holes Lily thought much too small to be of use to the large creature who had glared at them so balefully. Her father assured her that it was in the power of rats to make themselves fit into small places, that they were like yogis who know the secret of folding themselves down into suitcases. Lily plugged the holes with spoons of wet plaster. Now that her father believed in the creature's existence, he seemed unable to give it enough credence, and she had been elevated from the position of hysterical visionary to that of reliable reporter on the natural scene.

On Monday morning her father called his office to say he wasn't coming in. The sky was black with clouds, and flood predictions were easily come by; he used this as his excuse. Lily's mother called the school and said that she was ill and needed Lily at home. This easy lie shocked Lily, though she was glad of it. Then the three sat at the kitchen table and discussed their plans. They had sealed the rat in the kitchen; they were sure of this. And when next he appeared, he wouldn't find it easy to escape. The pots and pans sat out on the floor in little groups; all the food was set in boxes in the dining room. The cabinets stood open and empty. If he showed his face again there would be no place left to conceal it.

But though they sat at the table scanning the room for the better part of the morning, he took them by surprise. He appeared inside the cabinet beneath the sink, and none could say where he came from. Lily's father, who had armed himself with a hammer and a small axe, leaped to his feet and raced to the animal. By the time he had crossed the room the rat was gone. He fell on his knees and inspected every inch of the cabinet with his hands. "How the hell does he do it?" he said, and then, "Oh, this is it." Lily and her mother joined him and they all looked with wonder at the hole, which was really a broken flap in the plasterboard at the back of the cabinet. Behind it was another hole, smaller, ragged, and deep. It opened into darkness, and the outside edge of it was lined with a half inch of wood.

"Do you know what it is?" Lily's father asked.

"Why is it so dark?" she said, for it seemed to Lily that such a hole should open into daylight.

"Because it's inside a drawer," her father replied. He seemed immensely pleased with this pronouncement, like a detective who has discovered the long-sought final clue.

"The old dresser?" her mother said.

Her father stood up, gripping his gleaming axe, and started out the back door for the porch. Then Lily understood. On the porch there was a dresser in which, as a baby, she had kept her toys. It backed up against the house, against, she realized, this very cabinet. The rat had disappeared into the dark hole, but the dark hole was the inside of that dresser. Lily and her mother exchanged looks of mild surprise; then they too rushed out onto the porch. Her father stood poised before the dresser. "He's in there," he said. "I can hear him."

"Which drawer?" her mother asked.

"The middle, I think."

"What are you going to do?" Lily cried. She was suddenly desperately frightened.

"I'm going to open the drawer just a little and try to catch him in it." As he said this he squatted down, laying his axe near his feet and pulled the middle drawer open an inch. Lily could hear the scratching of the animal's claws against the wood. Another inch, she thought, and they would see his dreadful face. Her father pulled the drawer out carefully, leaning back a little so that his face wouldn't be near the opening. Now he could see into the drawer. Then, abruptly, he pulled the drawer all the way out and threw it down on the porch. Lily saw her old metal tea set scattered across the bottom, and there was a plastic strainer, which she had once used for sand, that flew out of the drawer when it hit the ground and rolled in a dizzy circle toward the screen. Except for that, the drawer was empty, and the space in the dresser where the drawer had been was empty as well.

"Did he go back in the kitchen?" her mother asked. The hole that had allowed the creature's easy entrance into their lives was now visible and they stood looking into it as their greatest oversight. They heard a scratching, then a thudding sound that came distinctly from the top drawer. The rat was trapped at last and he was frantic. Lily's father turned toward them. "Get back," he warned. Then he pulled the drawer out slowly, carefully, an inch, then another. Inside the drawer the rat was still, crouched, silent, as light flooded his last dark refuge.

Lily grasped her mother's hand and found it cold but willing to hold her own. Her father leaned over the dresser, placing one hand against the front of the drawer while with the other he began to pound on the top. Still there was no sound, no movement from inside the drawer.

"Is he in there?" Lily's mother asked. Her father turned his head to answer his wife and in that moment the rat made his move. He hit the front of the drawer with such force that her father's hand fell away, leaving the crack opened and unprotected. In the next instant the creature flew up before them, straight up; his legs battled the air like wings, his teeth were bared. He leaped straight at Lily's father, who staggered backward and put out his hands to stop this attack. But the rat caught him at the base of his throat, sinking his sharp teeth into the flesh and clinging to the shirt cloth with his fierce sharp claws.

Her father made a gasping sound and whirled around, clutching the animal at his throat. Lily saw his face — his eyes opened wide in shock, his teeth bared too now — in such a fury as she had never imagined. The rat clung to him as he fell to his knees, dropping one hand for the axe while the other closed over the animal's face. His fingers went inside the rat's mouth, prying the teeth from his flesh, and when he had pulled them free he raised the gray body over his head and dashed it to the floor. Then the rat screamed. It was the only sound he had made in the struggle, and his voice was high, clear, terror-stricken. Lily saw the oily edge of the axe blade as it came down through the air. She remembered how her father had sharpened and oiled it that morning in preparation for this blow.

The edge came down and Lily turned to her mother, who

was too stunned by what she saw to look away. There was the soft sound of flesh giving way, of small bones cracking, and it was quiet. When Lily looked back the rat was in two pieces, his head and forequarters on one side of the axe, his back legs and long tail severed completely and thrown a foot away by the force of the blade. Lily's father stood looking down at the sight, clutching his throat with one hand. He knew that the job was over, but his rage, Lily saw, was not yet under control. Her mother rushed to him, throwing her arms about him with a passion she had never shown him before and he held her against him tightly. Lily looked away, allowing her eyes their fill of the curiously rewarding sight of the rat's bisected body. His blood oozed out upon the boards from his wounds and from his open mouth, which was already stiffening with death. The wonder of his death afflicted her. A moment before he had threatened everything; now his harmless body lay before her, bereft of horror, only dull, large, gray, mysteriously still. She turned away from them all and went back into the kitchen. Her hands were sticky from fear and she washed them at the sink.

That night Lily slept fitfully. When she woke she could think of nothing but the rat, of how she had lain and listened to him as he came closer and closer. She sat up and looked about the room. Didn't she hear the scratching of his claws against the floor; wasn't that hushing sound caused by his breath? She lay back and turned to face the wall. Her mother had kissed her when she went to bed and her father had held her for a moment with warm confidence. She had touched the bandage on his neck tentatively. The doctor had suggested that the wound would become more painful before it began to heal. A rat bite, he told the family, was no joke, but there was no reason to expect complications. Her father had astounded the doctor with the story, keeping, as he talked, one hand resting protectively on his daughter's shoulder. He had, he was convinced, done what was necessary to set her fears at rest.

But now she was as full with fear as ever and she knew she wouldn't sleep. She got up and turned on the light in her bedroom; then she looked under the bed and in the closet. But not seeing anything didn't give her the rest she sought. At length she decided to go out, to take the plastic bag out of the garbage can, and look again on the remains of her enemy. She slipped on her robe, turned off her light, and went stealthily down the hall, passing her parents' bedroom door without a pause.

She opened the kitchen door, unlatched and opened the screen, and stepped out on the porch. The rain had stopped, and through the swiftly moving clouds the moon cast its desultory beams. Lily accustomed her eyes to the light and to the unexpected beauty of the scene before her. She focused her eyes on the moonflowers, like pools of milk among the dark leaves that covered the fence. The roses nearby raised their thorny branches, holding out papery leaves and flowers, gray and black, toward the sky. Her mother's vegetable garden fairly hummed with life, and, as she stood there, Lily thought of her mother and of how they had worked together one day, preparing the soil for the seeds.

Her mother had turned the soil with a shovel, and Lily, crouched barefoot in the dirt, had come behind her with a garden spade, breaking the big clods down with childish energy. She had stopped, then stood up and stepped forward into the rough dirt her mother had just turned. As her foot came down she noticed that the soil was warm; it invited her to press her toes into it. Lily looked at her feet and smiled, overcome with a delicious sensation. "What's funny?" her mother had asked and when Lily looked up she saw that her mother was smiling on her in the same way she smiled, sometimes, on her roses, with undisguised admiration.

"It's warm," Lily said. "Underneath. You should take off your shoes."

Her mother's smile had deepened and she indicated her shod foot, which rested on the wing of the shovel, with a look that explained her dilemma: she couldn't dig barefoot. Then she bent down and pressed her hand into the dirt near Lily's feet. She dug her fingers down and came up with a handful of the dark soil. She studied it intently for a moment, sifting it through her fingers. She had lectured Lily that morning on this chore and made it clear that the preparation of the soil was the most important work they would do that day. Everything, by which Lily understood her to mean the future of the garden, depended on its being done right. Now it was Lily's turn to smile, for she saw that her mother couldn't take her mind off the importance she attached to doing this work correctly. It was true, her fingers told her, the soil was warm, but her fingers asked a more penetrating question: would it yield?

Lily paused, examining this memory as she stood on the porch in the warm night air, and she shook her head slowly, affectionately, at the thought of her mother's passionate gardening. The fruit of that passion stood before her: tomatoes and eggplants heavy on their vines, lettuce like great balls of pearl, luminous in the darkness, the airy greens of the carrots, rustling continuously with the movement of the air, the black tangle of the green peas, climbing skyward on their tall tubes of screen. The scent of the mint and parsley bed rose to Lily and the sweetness of the air drew her out toward the steps. She looked down at the drawers of the old dresser, which lay scattered on the porch. Her mother had washed them furiously, as if to wash away the evidence of a desecration. Then Lily thought of the rat and she looked toward the garbage can with a sensation of dismay. It would be, she thought, foolish and unnecessary trouble to pull out his corpse now. She could consult her memory for a fresh, distinct, and detailed picture of his death; she could see, in her mind's eye, the blood darkening around his mouth, the dullness of his dead eyeballs. She wasn't certain that he wouldn't seek her out again, but, she thought, he would never again seek her in that particular form. His menace had quite gone out of that form; she had seen it with her own eyes. Her father had discarded the pieces of the rat's body without anger; he had even commented on the creature's remarkable size, taking, Lily had observed, some comfort in having defeated so formidable an enemy. Now that he was a danger to no one, the rat possessed the power to be marvelous.

Lily turned away, pushing her hair back from her face. She had told her mother she wanted her hair cut off and, to her surprise, had received no objection. But now this seemed an unnecessary precaution. She returned to her bed, possessed of a strange fearlessness; it was as insistent as her own heartbeat, and as she drifted off to sleep it swelled and billowed within her and she understood, for the first time, that she was safe.

The Way of the World

I WAS ELEVEN; she was twenty-five, thirty at the most. She was tall, thin, well dressed, pale skin, pale eyes, pale hair; she gave an impression of light. But there were dark shadows beneath those limpid eyes and she had the jaded, distracted look of someone who hasn't slept well in days. As soon as I saw her pulling her thin suitcase wearily down the crowded aisle toward me, I knew she was running away from something bad. She surveyed her fellow passengers coldly, no doubt looking for two empty seats, but as that wasn't possible she took the aisle seat next to mine. She got on at some little town in Mississippi and she was with me all the way to Kansas City.

I was pleased when she sat next to me, because I thought she looked elegant and exotic and, of course, because she was a woman, which meant I didn't have to be afraid of her. She said a few words to me as she settled her cheap suitcase in place. I think she asked me where I was going. Her voice was a disappointment — coarse, cold, though she was clearly making an effort to be civil. She wasn't in the seat five minutes before she fell asleep.

She slept for hours. I watched her sleeping for so long that I began to feel close to her, as if we were friends in this powerful, deep sleep. She seemed vulnerable, and that made me want to protect her. I was a child but I knew she was more delicately situated than I was. My purse had plenty of money in it, the porter had been slipped a ten-dollar bill to keep an eye on me, and my adored and adoring grandmother would be waiting for me in the morning when we got to Kansas City. Somehow I knew this pretty woman was having no such luck.

At noon the porter came around with sandwiches. I was pleased when I heard him coming along the aisle, chatting with the other passengers in his nosy, slightly officious way, because I thought he would wake up my lady. But she didn't hear him; she didn't hear anything. I bought a sandwich for myself and another for her and two Cokes. I stashed this food away in my canvas bag and waited. Sooner or later she had to wake up.

How I loved the long train ride into the night. Usually I was with my older sister and we prowled from car to car, played cards in the club car, and ate fresh rainbow trout in the dining car. This year she had opted for summer camp and, after some long-distance trepidations, my mother had been persuaded to send me to my grandmother alone. My fantasy life was so powerful and complete that this meant I was to spend twenty-six hours at the center of a marvelous drama, that the whole train, unknown to anyone on it, was mine, and that I could create myself on it any way I pleased.

Later, on other trips, I would tell lies about myself to the other passengers. I would pretend to be a leukemia victim en route to my doctor, or the child of a stricken opera star, crossing a continent to see my mother's last performance, but on that trip, my first alone, I became, in spite of my best efforts, the property of the woman who had chosen a seat next to mine.

I remember today, thirty years later, exactly the care I took in stepping over her to get into the aisle. I walked along, glancing at the other passengers, who were sleeping or reading, until I got to the bathroom. I was strangely anxious, bored with sitting next to the sleeping woman, but unwilling to leave her in case she woke up. In the shiny, compact, spotless bathroom I looked at myself in the mirror for a long time. My plain little face looked back at me woefully. Where was the beautiful little girl inside? When would everyone be able to see her as clearly as I did? I tried fluffing my hair out, turning my face a little to give myself a sidelong glance, such as I had seen beautiful women give in films, but it wasn't the same.

When I got back, the lady was awake, looking sleepily into space. She didn't notice me until I stood next to her, waiting for her to let me into my seat. "Oh," she said, moving her long legs aside. "Sorry." I sat down and looked out the window, my tongue like a knot in my mouth. Now was the time to tell her about the sandwiches, but I doubted I had the courage to bring up any subject. I sneaked a look at her. She gave off an air of fatigue, of hopelessness, looking vacantly into space. I thought she was the most exhausted person I had ever seen.

At last I began rummaging in my bag and brought out one of the sandwiches. It was big, made with French bread, lots of ham, American cheese, lettuce and tomato, wrapped in sticky plastic wrap. I began struggling with the wrapping, feeling her eyes on my hands. I was speechless with embarrassment, but I raised my eyes to hers. She was looking right at me, not smiling, not friendly at all, really, but vacant. Somehow I found my voice. "I got one for you," I said, reaching down to my bag and fishing out the other sandwich. "You were sleeping."

She took the sandwich and held it in her lap a moment, uncertainly. "Thanks," she said. Then she looked back at me and said, coldly, as if I'd done something annoying, "I can't pay you for it."

"Oh, that's all right," I said quickly. "I've got plenty of money."

"Oh," she said.

I started digging in my bag again. "I got some Cokes too," I said, pulling out one, then the other. "They're not too cold anymore. I can get us some ice from the diner." In my nervousness I had rewrapped my sandwich, so I slipped it back into the bag and stood up.

"All right," she said, making room for me to pass. As I walked away I could hear her unwrapping the crinkly plastic wrap. Good, I thought, she's going to eat it.

In the diner I got the ice, two bags of potato chips, two apples, and two oatmeal cookies. When I got back to my lady she'd eaten half of her sandwich. She moved aside for me quickly and I sat down with a thump, balancing as well as I could the heavy cardboard tray they'd given me. I pulled down the seat tray and started taking out my supplies. "I got this other stuff for us too," I said. Still she did not smile, but she gave me a look of approval that filled me with inexplicable happiness. I'd done the right thing.

We turned our attention to our food. I was amazed at how much my lady ate and how rapidly. My sandwich was too big for me, so I offered her half. "Are you sure," she said, but she had already reached out to take it. She managed to make everything disappear without seeming greedy. She wasn't stuffing it down, as I'd seen hungry children at my school do; she just ate steadily, with the same tired, vacant indifference that characterized her every gesture. It fascinated me, and as she didn't seem to care how much I looked at her, I took her in as steadily as she took in the food I'd given her.

When she was finished, we stuffed the wrappings into the tray. "Thanks," she said. "I was really hungry." I was too shy to respond. I concentrated on making a place for the tray on the floor, then on taking out a book, which I pretended to read for a few minutes. My lady sat beside me, very still. After turning several pages I summoned the courage to look up at her again. She had pushed her seat back and she reclined against it as if she had been thrown there, gazing into the space above her with an expression of mild hopelessness. As I watched, she sat up, opened her purse, and extracted a pair of sunglasses. She put these on without so much as glancing in my direction, then fell back against the seat.

She's running away from a man, I thought.

How did I know that? I tried to concentrate on my book but the revelation that had just come to me was too disturbing. I let the pages fall closed in my lap and looked out the window at the stream of green and brown that was the countryside of Arkansas. Now and then a cow or horse hurtled by; there were no people in sight. I felt weary, jaded; the wonderful trip had lost its magic. I was an ordinary little girl after all. By shifting my focus I could see my own ordinary face in the window glass, with the scenery running right through it. I fell into my habitual frame of mind, a dreamy, semiconsciousness so hard to penetrate that I often forgot where I was. My lady rode along beside me, silent, blind, still, like a mysterious guide to the underworld.

Where was that underworld? I can scarcely recall it. What were the daydreams of that plain little girl? I know she never thought about anything but herself, that she was constantly creating an alternate self because the reality of her complete powerlessness was too painful to bear. What she knew about the lady on the train must have come through some intuition, for she wasn't an observant child, and the world of adults scarcely interested her.

What interested her was a recurring dream, connected to reality by a narrow flight of stairs. The stairs were in a neighbor's house, and at the top of the stairs was a room belonging to the neighbor's eldest daughter, a pouting, belligerent, vain adolescent who was rumored to be "wild" and to have some dangerous relations with certain boys in the neighborhood. The little girl on the train had never been inside that room; it was off-limits. Instead, in a dream, time and time again, she climbed those stairs and opened the door to find the black velvet chamber. The heavy velvet covered everything and poured off the walls and over the floor like waves of black water on a moonless night. Light came from somewhere, though there were no windows and no furniture; a reddish light suffused the blackness like a fog. It was magical, erotic. The room beckoned the dreaming child night after night. She stood in the open doorway unable to take a step in any direction.

The room was part of a waking dream as well. The child was in the center of this dream, but she wasn't a child. She was a beautiful, fair-haired, voluptuous young woman, dressed in a robe of flowing white. Two men led her along a hall, and there were other men too, looking out the doorways into the hall. Behind these men were rooms, all draped in brocades, strange tapestries, thickly carpeted, dark and as soundless as the young woman who was led along to a final door. Her hands were tied behind her back; the men led her by her elbows. Behind the last door was the black velvet chamber, and this time she would be forced to go inside whether she wanted to or not.

Strange little creature, lost in a fantasy, how she looked and looked at her own face in the window, lost in her dream of another world while the train rattled on into her future. For a moment I can stop that train, freeze it all in time and space, and see her sitting there, her timid dreams frozen in her eyes.

On another train, en route to a city the dreaming child never heard of, is another little girl, the same age, on her first train trip alone. This trip is only an hour and a half long, from New Haven to Springfield. Just ahead of that train is the platform and in a few moments the train will arrive. I've been on the platform for five minutes now, with a few other people who are waiting to get on. I'm the only one waiting to pick someone up. The station master told me to come up here because the conductor would not release my daughter until he saw me. I'm pleased with Amtrak. They've taken better care of her than I'd expected. I can hear the train whistle now, not like a whistle but a wail, like a long cry of pain. It's a sound that is oddly comforting. I know my little girl and I imagine she is between the cars now, for the train is slowing down and she will be moving her suitcase to get off first, and I know that she is listening to the whistle too, but she listens with that unprejudiced sense of wonder, that deep, helpless listening we forget over the years, listening to the train howling into the cold, black, indifferent universe, listening down to the bones.

That other little girl, the one who lives in a dream, the

one who has been touched briefly by the sharp, cold, unexpected finger of reality in the form of a woman running
away from trouble, that little girl hardly ever listens to anything. She stares into the window while the train rushes
through the rest of a dull summer evening, longing to see a
face I know will never be there. Mine is the face that will
eventually look back at her. Far away, down the years, I'm
looking at her now.

Sea Lovers

On moonless nights the sea is black. Ships sail upon it and shine their lights through the double blackness of water and air. The darkness swallows up light like a great yawning snake. On the beach people walk, looking out to sea, but there is no sign of the ships, no sign of the drowning sailors, no sign of anything living or dead, only the continual rushing and ebbing of water sucking and sucking at the shoreline, drawing the innocent, foolish lovers out a little farther. They are unafraid, showing each other their courage. They laugh, pointing to the water. No one can see them. They slip off their clothes and wade in. The waves draw them out, tease them, lick upward slowly about her pale thighs, slap him playfully, dashing a little salt spray into his eyes. He turns to her, she to him; they can scarcely see each other, but they are strong swimmers and they link hands as they go out a little farther, a little deeper. Now the waves swell about them and they embrace. She is losing her footing, so she leans against him, allows the rising water to lift her right off her feet as she is pressed against him. He pulls her in tightly, laughing into her mouth as he kisses her.

They can't be seen; they can't be heard. The people on the shore will find their clothes, but they will never find the lovers. A solitary mermaid passing nearby hears their laughter and pauses. She watches them, but even her strange fish-pale eyes can barely see them; the night is so black, so moonless. She could sing to them, as she has sung to other drowning mortals, but she is weary tonight and her heart is heavy from too much solitude. She has not seen another of her kind for many months. She was nearly killed a few days ago, swimming near a steamship. Her head is full of the giant engine blades, of that moment when she looked up and saw that she was a hair's-breadth from death. That was when she turned toward shore. She is swimming in with the tide, even as the lovers are sucked out and down. When she drops beneath the surface of the water, the mermaid can just see the woman's long hair billowing out around her face. Her mouth is open wide in a silent scream. Oh yes, the mermaid thinks, if she could be heard it would be quite a racket. People would come running for miles. But the sea filled her mouth before the sound could get out and no one will ever hear her now. She clings to the man, and he, in his panic, pushes her away. This started out as such a lark. It was a calm, hot, black night and the white sands of the beach made all the light there was. They had wandered along, stopping to kiss and tease, laughing, so happy, so safe, and now this: she was drowning and he could not save her. Worse, worse, she would pull him under.

The mermaid rises above the crest of a wave and looks back at them. She sees only one pale hand reaching up, the fingers splayed and tense, as if reaching for something to hold; then the water closes over that too.

The sea is full of death, now more than ever. The mermaid

has, twice in her short life, found herself swimming in a sea red with blood: once from a whale struck by a steamship, once from men drowning during a war. Their ship had been torpedoed and most of them were bleeding when they hit the water. The sharks had done the rest. That time she had dived beneath the battle, for the noise was deafening and the light from the explosions dazzled her so that she could scarcely see. One of the men clutched at her as she swam away, but she shook him off. She disliked being seen by men, even when they were about to die. She could amuse herself singing to them when they couldn't see her, when they were wild-eyed and desperate, clinging to a broken spar from a boat shattered by a storm, or treading water in that ridiculous way they had, with those pathetic, useless legs; then she would hide among the waves and sing to them. Sometimes it made them more frantic, but a few times she had seen a strange calm overtake a drowning man, so that his struggles became more mechanical, less frantic, and he simply stayed afloat as long as he could and went under at last quietly, without that panicked gagging and struggling that was so disgusting to see. Once a man had died like that very near her, and she had felt so curious about him that she drifted too close to him, and in the last moment of his life he saw her. His eyes were wide open and startled already from his long, bitter struggle with death; he knew he was beaten yet could not give up. He saw her and he reached out to her, his mouth opened as if he would speak, but it was blood and not words that poured over his lips and she knew even as he did that he was gone. She had, by her nature, no sympathy for men, but this one interested her.

It was a cold, calm night and the man was so far from land that it would be days before his body was tossed up, bloated, unrecognizable, on some shore. He had been sailing alone in a small boat, far out to sea; she had, in fact, been watching his progress for days. The storm that had wrecked his little craft was intense, but quickly over, and he had survived it somehow, holding on to pieces of the wreckage. Then it was a few days of hopeless drifting for him. She watched from a distance, listened to him when he began to babble to himself. Near the end he stunned her by bursting into song, singing as loud as he could, though he had little strength left, a lively song that she couldn't understand. When he was dead she did something she had never done: she touched him. His skin was strange, he was already stiffening, and she was fascinated by the feel of it. She took him by the shoulders and brought him down with her, down where the water was still and clear, and there she looked at him carefully. His eyes fascinated her, so different from her own. She discovered the hard nails on his fingers and toes. She examined his mouth, which she thought incredibly ugly, and his genitals, which confused her. Gradually a feeling of revulsion overtook her and she swam away from him abruptly, leaving him wedged in a bed of coral and kelp, food for the bigger fish that might pass his way.

Now she remembers him as she swims toward shore, and her thin upper lip curls back at the thought of him. She is being driven toward land by a force stronger than her own will, and she hates that force even as she gives in to it, just as she hated the dead man.

It is dark and the air is still. Though the sea is never still, she has the illusion of calm. She swims effortlessly just beneath the surface of the waves. She is getting close to shore, dangerously close, but she neither slows nor alters her course.

She is acquainted with many stories that tell of the perils

of the land, stories similar to the ones men tell about the sea, full of terror, wonder, magic, and romance. The moral of these tales (that she can no more live on land than men can live in the sea) has not escaped her. She has seen the land; she knows about its edges and she has seen mountains rising above the surface of the water. Sometimes there are people on these mountains, walking about or driving in their cars. This coast, which she must have chosen, is flat and long. There is white sand along it for miles and behind the sand a line of green, though in the darkness its vivid colors are only black before white before gray. The mermaid can scarcely look at it. She is caught up in the surf that moves relentlessly toward land. For a while she can drop beneath the waves, but soon the water is too shallow, and when her tail and side scrape against the hard sand at the bottom she shudders as if death had reached up suddenly and touched her. The waves smash her down and roll her over. Her tail wedges into the sand and sends a cloud over her; she feels the grit working in under her scales. She raises her webbed hands to wipe it away. It is different from the sand in the deep water; it feels sharp and somehow more irritating and it smells of land.

It's useless to fight the waves. She lets her body rise and fall with them, rolling in with the surf as heavy and un-resisting as a broken ship or a dead man. Soon there is nothing but sand beneath her, and the water ebbs away, leaving her helpless, exposed to the warm and alien air. The pounding she has taken has left her barely conscious. She lies on her stomach in the sand, her arms stretched out over her head, her face turned to one side so that what little water there is can flow over it. Her long silvery body writhes in the shallows and she is aghast with pain. From the waist down she is numb and she lifts her head as best she can to look back at herself. She can hardly feel her tail, rising and falling in the sand, working her in deeper and deeper, against her will. It is horrible, and she is so helpless that she falls back down with a groan. Something is seeping out of her, spilling out into the sand. It is slippery and viscous; at first she thinks she is bleeding, then she imagines it is her life. She moans again and struggles to lift herself, pushing her hands against the sand. She opens and closes her mouth, gasping for water. Her skin is drying out; it burns along her back, her shoulders, her neck. She presses her face down as a little trickle of water rushes up near her, but it is not enough and she manages only to get more damp sand in her mouth. She lifts her head and shoulders once more against the un-expected weight of the air, and as she does, she sees the man.

He is running toward her. He has left his fishing gear to the whims of the sea and he is running toward her as fast as he can. Her heart sinks. He is in his element and she is at his mercy. But in the next heartbeat she is struck with cunning and a certainty that flashes up in her consciousness with the force of memory. In the same moment she knows that her lower body is now her own, and strength surges through her like an electric current. He must not see her face; she knows this. She spreads her hair out over her shoulders and hides her face in the sand. Her body is still, her strong tail lies flat in the shallows, as shiny and inert as a sheet of steel.

She listens to the slap of his bare feet against the hard wet sand as he comes closer. Soon she can hear his labored breathing and his mumbled exclamations, though his words are meaningless to her. This is a big catch, but it will be a while before he understands what he has caught. In the darkness he takes her for a woman, and it is not until he is bending over her that he sees the peculiar unwomanly shape of her lower body. For a moment he thinks she is a woman who has been half devoured by an enormous fish. He looks back at the shore, as if help might come from it, but there is no help for him now. His hands move over her shoulders. He is determined to pull her out of the water, not for any reason but that she has washed up on the shore and that is what men do with creatures who wash up on the shore. "My God," he says, and the pitch of his voice makes the mermaid clench her jaw, "are you still alive?"

She does not move. His hands are communicating all sorts of useless information to him: this creature is very like a woman, and though her smooth skin is extraordinarily cold, it is soft, supple, alive. His fingers dig in under her arms and lift her a little. She is careful to keep her face down, hidden in the stream of her long hair. This hair, he can see even in the darkness, is almost white, thick, unnaturally long; it falls voluptuously over her shoulders. He is losing his grip; she is heavier than he imagined, and he releases her for a moment while he changes his position. He straddles her back now. She hears the squish of his feet as he steps over her head and positions himself behind her. As he does he takes a closer look at her long back and sees the line where the pale skin turns to silver. "What are you?" he says, but he doesn't pause to find out. His hands are under her arms again; one of them strays over her breasts quickly, momentarily, as he lifts her. Her heart is beating furiously now so that she can hear nothing else. For one second she hangs limp in his arms and in the next she comes alive.

She brings her arms quickly under her and pushes up so suddenly and with such force that the man loses his balance and falls over her. She is, thanks to the sea, several times as strong as he is, and she has no difficulty now turning over beneath him. He struggles, astounded at the sudden powerful fury of the creature he had intended to save, but he struggles in vain. They are entwined together in the sand, rising and falling like lovers, but the man, at least, is aware that this is not love. Her strong arms close around him and he can feel her cold clawed hands in his hair. His face is wedged against her shoulder, and as he breathes in the peculiar odor of her skin, he is filled with terror. She takes a handful of his hair and pulls his head up so that she can look at him and he at her. What he sees paralyzes him, as surely as if he had looked at Medusa, though it is so dark he can see only the glitter of her cold, flat, lidless eyes, the thin hard line of her mouth, which opens and closes beneath his own. He can hear the desperate sucking sound fish make when they are pulled from the sea. She rolls him under her as easily as if he were a woman and she a man. With one hand she holds his throat while with the other she tears away the flimsy swimming trunks, all the protection he had against her. Her big tail is moving rapidly now, pushing her body up over his. Her hand loosens at his throat and he gasps for air, groaning, pushing against her with all his strength, trying to push her away. She raises herself on her arms, looking down at him curiously and he sees the sharp fish teeth, the dry black tongue. Her tail is powerful and sinuous; it has come up between his legs like an eel and now the sharp edge of it grazes the inside of his thighs. It cuts him; he can feel the blood gathering at the cuts, again and again, each time a little closer to the groin. He cries out, but no one hears him. The mermaid doesn't even bother to look at him as she brings her tail up hard against his testicles and slices through the unresisting flesh, once, twice, three times; that's all it takes. His fingers have torn the skin on her back and he has bitten into her breast so that she is bleeding, but she can't feel anything as pain now. She drops back over him and clasps his throat between her hands, pressing hard and for a long time until he ceases to struggle.

Then she is quiet but not still. Carefully she takes up the bleeding pocket of flesh from between his legs; carefully cradling it in her hands, she transfers it into the impression she left in the sand before this struggle began. The sea will wash it all away in a minute or two, for the tide is coming in, but that's all the time she needs. She pushes the sand up around this bloody treasure; then, exhausted and strangely peaceful, she rolls away into the shallows. The cool water revives her and she summons her strength to swim out past the breakers. Now she can feel the pain in her back and her breast, but she can't stop to attend to it. As soon as the water is deep enough she dives beneath the waves, and as she does her tail flashes silver in the dark night air; like great metal wings, the caudal fin slices first the air, then the water.

On the shore everything is still. The waves are creeping up around the man, prying him loose from the sand. Little water fingers rush in around his legs, his arms, his face. Already the water has washed his blood away. Farther down the beach his fishing gear floats in the rising water. His tackle box has spilled its insides; all his lures and hooks, all the wiles he used to harvest the sea, bob gaily on the waves.

Farther still I am walking on the shore with my lover. We have been dancing at a party. The beach house is behind us, throwing its white light and music out into the night air as if it could fill the void. Inside it was hot, bright; we couldn't hear the waves or smell the salt air, and so we are feeling lightheaded and pleased with ourselves for having had the good sense to take a walk. We are walking away from the house and away from the dead man, but not away from the sea. I've taken my shoes off so that I can let the water cool my tired feet. My lover follows my example; he sheds his shoes and stops to roll up his pants legs. As I stand looking out into the black water and the blacker sky it seems to me that I can see tiny lights, like stars, flashing in the waves. "What are those lights?" I ask him when he joins me, and he looks but says he doesn't see any lights.

"Mermaids," I say. I could almost believe it. I raise my hand and wave at them. "Be careful," I say. "Stay away from the shore." My lover is very close to me. His arms encircle me; he draws me close to him. The steady pounding of the waves and the blackness of the night excite us. We would like to make love in the sand, at the water's edge.

The Woman Who Was Never Satisfied

THE TELLER could see it in her eyes and in the way she drew the money from him, carelessly, her fingertips touching his hand: she was never satisfied. She looked up apologetically. Her eyes were wide, clear, cold, and, with her full lips perpetually parted (she suffered from allergies and a sinus condition and used her mouth for breathing), she had the expression of having just received an electrical shock.

There was no one behind her at the window. The teller had the opportunity to watch her as she turned from him and crossed the cavernous lobby of the bank. She sat down on one of the velvet couches, her purse in her lap, her hands folded upon her purse, and looked up and down the long room. She didn't appear to be thinking of anything or looking for anyone, but rather to be practicing the outward appearance of self-possession, which a glance at her pale eyes belied, for she had the expression of an animal in danger. She was looking for a way out.

Presently a man entered the lobby, cast a quick look about the room, and went to stand before her couch. She looked up at him, the corners of her mouth lifting into a nervous smile.

Because he stood so close to her, she was unable to rise, so she looked back down at her purse. Her fingers pressed the leather with enough force to leave damp impressions. The man stepped back. "Are you ready?" he inquired.

She nodded, stood up, and followed him, a step behind, to the street.

It was true that she was never satisfied, but it was not because she expected that she might be. In fact she believed that as far as men were concerned, she never would be. Her interest in her companion was superficial at best, and what she required of him was so insignificant that her failures were always the result of requiring too little, so little that it was insulting. But she was inured to the vanity of her lovers and shrugged them off like ill-fitting garments.

Outside, the man put his arm around her shoulder and kissed her neck just below her ear. "Eva," he said, "are you ready?"

She smiled, looking past his eyes. She offered him her mouth but not her eyes, as if she were distracted. He allowed his hand to slip down her arm, pulling her body in close to his.

Lately she had come to think that what she wanted was something momentary. She found this notion made life a good deal more bearable, for any moment could be the one, and it was important to search each one, to turn it inside out, to be sure. Her state of expectancy was more intense during certain intervals; for example, from the moment this man had joined her to that in which he would leave her, it was very intense indeed. But occasionally, when she was alone, she felt a sense of urgency that overwhelmed her, and she wondered if whatever it was that was coming toward her might not arrive when she was alone. It could be, she thought, no more than a remarkable idea.

Her husband, whom she had loved in an indulgent fashion, for he was ten years younger than she and she had never succeeded in taking him seriously, had perished in an automobile accident. Eva had not escaped injury. She had no memory of the accident, but when she regained consciousness in the hospital she had been possessed of an obsessive interest in the fate of the two snakes that had been in the back seat of the car. Her husband was a zoologist; the snakes were being taken to a veterinarian. They were each over four feet long, and Lawrence had held one up for her inspection before putting them into the car. Eva had gazed with admiration at the flat black eye, the flickering tongue. "What's wrong with her?" she had inquired.

"Him," her husband corrected her. "I'm damned if I know. He won't eat."

He had set the wooden boxes carefully in the back seat, improvising a brace in front to keep them from sliding about. When the police opened the car after the accident, the boxes were there. They had been jammed together by the force of the crash, and several of the thin boards had snapped. The snakes were gone. Eva, as she lay beneath the onslaught of another shot of morphine, became convinced that they had escaped into her imagination. There they lay, cold-blooded and dangerous, dying from lack of nourishment and beautiful in their indifference to death.

"Here, Eva," the man said, steering her into a doorway. Then he took her hand and led her into an elevator. She stood looking out at the lobby of the hotel; it was one of a chain, and the décor was as impersonal as a postage stamp. There was always that touch of red, in a chair or a rug or in the wallpaper. To remind us of our blood, she thought as the elevator doors closed and she found herself looking at a panel of red, edged in gold. There was no one else in the elevator, and she expected the man to take advantage of this solitude, but he didn't. They stood together, their eyes raised to the ascending legend of numbers over the door. The man had pushed the button 7 and when the number 7 lit, the doors opened. They stepped out, the man fishing in his coat pocket for a key, which, Eva observed, was abnormally large and heavy. Once this had been a very expensive and exclusive hotel. All that remained of that place, she thought, was the keys.

She had spent two months in the hospital after the accident. Fortunately, her husband had been well insured. He was buried before she regained consciousness. His family took over all his affairs with an efficiency that struck her, when she was well enough to observe it, as indecent. There was nothing for her to do but lie in the hospital in the pale haze the morphine dragged over her consciousness. For a month she was as calm as death. Then they began to reduce the dosage and Eva was aware at last of being miserably ill. Her hair fell out in handfuls, her eyes watered and burned, her gums bled, she chewed her fingernails to the quick. One morning, when she had fifteen minutes to wait before the nurse brought her the injection she had been craving for an hour, her husband's mother came in and asked her what she wanted done with the house. "It's very expensive," her mother-in-law said apologetically. "They've taken all the animals, so the place is empty. I can have the furniture put in storage for you. It's such a big place. When you get well . . ."

"Close it up," Eva said. "Sell everything."

"If that's what you want."

Eva tried to drink water from the glass on the nightstand but she was unable to control her trembling hands. Her mother-in-law looked away. She realized she hadn't the courage to ask them to keep the black dog for her, her husband's favorite dog. "You've always hated me," she said.

The older woman continued to gaze at her hands. "You're ill," she said. "You're imagining things."

Eva laughed. "Can't you get out? Can't you leave me alone?"

"Don't worry about the house," her mother-in-law said as she was leaving. "I'll take care of everything."

A month later, when Eva left the hospital, she didn't know where she was going. But her wallet was full of credit cards, so she didn't experience the embarrassment of being able to go nowhere; it was only that she didn't know what she wanted. She stood in the parking lot and looked back at the window of her hospital room, where, doubtless, the bed was already filled. She wished that she could have morphine, for the sun was too bright in her face and when she looked in her purse for the Valium the nurse had given her, the sight of her own hands filled her with despair. She could think of no one to call. She had a brother, but he was always busy and so absorbed by his family that he treated her as a witness to his success. She took a cab to a hotel and when she was safe in her room, she lay across the bed and thought about the snakes. They may have made it across the highway. Had they gone in the same direction?

Without ever having willed it, she was entirely free; her life was her own. Once she had sworn that nothing less would do. Now her freedom sounded as hollow and useless as the inside of her own head, where, she thought, her brain had shrunken into a small, damp, palpitating ball. She closed her eyes. At last, she thought. Everything is quiet and still. She thought of her husband. She tried to remember his face but couldn't bring it into focus, so she lay there naming his features — his mouth, his nose, his eyes, which she knew so well — but no image came to her. She thought of the photographs she had of him, but they were all in the house. And the house was gone. She was aware of how completely unsatisfactory everything would be now, of how difficult it would be to find any pleasure, any peace, and she knew that now she would be as she had been before, always looking, always waiting, always in a state of vicious expectancy.

Now the man put the key in the lock and pushed the door open before her. She stood looking into the hotel room and she thought that from that vantage it looked very appealing, so clean, so bright. The man pressed his hand against the base of her spine and she stepped forward. He followed her and put his arms around her, pulling her back against his chest and caressing her neck, her ear, with his dry lips. She fought a wave of revulsion, an impulse to push him away. He turned her toward him and she didn't resist. "Eva," he said, kissing her eyelids. She opened her eyes when his mouth closed over her own and looked at his eyelids with a feeling of helplessness, for she saw that what was to follow would not contain that satisfaction she longed for, and she felt that after this failure she might be discouraged enough to stop trying. And if she could stop trying, then, she thought, everything would be so simple.

Before her marriage she had discovered a bizarre and temporary cure for her insatiability. She had a job then, but it required only half her attention. Her head buzzed with ideas and she was often so nervous that she stuttered. She consulted a doctor, who suggested various tests, one of which required her to sit in a room for eight hours while a nurse took periodic samples of her blood. She had not eaten the day before, and as the hours passed and the vials of blood filled the nurse's rack, she began to feel remarkably calm. By the time she left the building, she was convinced that she had found a cure for her condition.

The tests showed that her blood was not, in its make-up, suspect, but she knew the truth. Two months later she went to another doctor, gave the same complaint, and was scheduled for another eight-hour test. The nurse was awkward this time, continually missing her veins and leaving her arm swollen and bruised, but on the elevator, as she listened to the silence inside her skull, she decided that such peace was worth any price.

At the same time, Eva knew this behavior was unthinkable, and she wished to stop. She made an appointment with a psychologist a friend had recommended. He was, she was told, good with obsessives.

And so he was. She talked to him for six weeks and he understood her perfectly. In the seventh week he began their sessions by producing a hypodermic syringe from his desk drawer. She followed him obediently to the bathroom and looked at her own face in the mirror as he withdrew three or four tubes of blood, which he discharged unceremoniously into the sink drain. After this he made love to her on the rug for twenty minutes and spent the last thirty minutes listening in rapt attention to her halfhearted description of how she had come to this most wretched pass in her life.

But she couldn't afford him and finally had to give him up. Nor could she find another man to replace him without pay. Instead she met her husband and saw in his clear and innocent gaze the unexpected possibility of salvation.

She met him at a party. Her date, who was her employer,

had left her to attend a conversation on the other side of the room. She sat on a couch looking about uncertainly, and her gaze came to rest upon Lawrence, who stood leaning against a bookcase, his head inclined peculiarly toward the breast pocket of his coat, his large hand poised midair in its journey to that pocket, an eyedropper of yellow liquid clenched between thumb and forefinger. As she watched, he squeezed the liquid into his pocket, his brow knit over his task. She was so curious, she couldn't look away, and when he cast a hurried and guilty look about the room he saw her staring. A few moments later he sat down beside her on the couch. "You see what I have," he said, opening his coat. She looked into the pocket and saw a small naked creature with sealed eyes and a damp black nose.

"What is it?" she asked.

"It's a squirrel." He smiled at the animal benignly. "A baby. I have to feed him every twenty minutes, so I brought him along."

She looked again at the tiny animal. The sight of it sleeping at a party of humans made her feel unexpectedly gay. Then she looked into the clear eyes of the man.

"My name is Lawrence," he said. "I didn't want you to think I was crazy."

She never tried to defend herself against him, because he was so much younger and because of all the men she had ever known he was the most friendly. His passion was for animals, for keeping them alive. This fascinated Eva, who recalled a persistent childhood fantasy, one in which she lived among wild animals and neither had nor desired human companionship. She had always kept pets when she could, when her landlords or her lovers would stand for it, and she admired anyone who had the courage to commit his energies to nature. When she first visited Lawrence's house, it was as if her childhood dream had come insanely true. There were animals everywhere — monkeys, dogs, cats, rabbits, birds of every description, mice, gerbils, squirrels, and fish. In the yard there were horses, cows, goats, and a sheep. Lawrence stood in the midst of this menagerie with a look of distraction, for he wanted Eva to share a bed on which two cats and a dog were sleeping companionably. The activity in the room was ceaseless as Eva pulled back the spread and sat down to pull off her shoes.

"Does all this noise put you off?" he inquired.

"No," she said, drawing him down beside her. "I like it."

She liked it so well she couldn't leave. Lawrence needed all the help he could get and was willing to teach her what he knew. Their marriage was the outcome of a necessary partnership. She discovered that she was really what she had imagined she might be, one of the rare and fortunate people who can live with animals. She liked getting up in the night to drop boiled egg yolk down the straining throat of an impatient bluejay. She liked rocking a sick Diana monkey and coaxing him into taking a teaspoon of medicine. She liked the constant upheaval as well animals returned to the zoo and sick animals arrived in Lawrence's sympathetic arms. She paid no attention to the things she didn't like, the hair on her clothes and in her food, the necessity to drop perfectly live mice into the glassed-in dens of large and ravenous snakes, the constant duties of maintenance, the difficulty of getting even a minimum of sleep. Most of all, she found, she liked Lawrence. He was energetic and intelligent, and possessed, where Eva was concerned, remarkably good timing. He knew when to leave her alone, when to treat her passionately, when to hold her with the same curious sympathy he lavished upon his sick animals. She was not unhappy and found she needed all her blood to manage a day's work. She told Lawrence very little about herself.

Two years passed and then there was the morning when she helped him load the big snakes into the car and got in beside him. He smiled at her and brushed her lips with the back of his hand. They drove away from the house in a good humor. Eva looked back to see one of the goats resolutely slamming his horns against a fence post.

She wondered how long it would have lasted. Wasn't his timing, once more, exactly right? Didn't the car swerve off the road at just the moment she had framed the wish that Lawrence and all his animals were dead? And he left her so well provided that she needn't work. She could do as she pleased, if she could ever find anything to please her again.

The man had removed her blouse and attached his mouth to her left breast. She felt nauseated. She pushed him away and to his look of hurt surprise addressed her weakest smile. "Could we do it now?" she said. "Before. My head is spinning."

He straightened, releasing her. "If you like."

"Please," she said, turning away. She went into the bathroom and sat on the edge of the tub. He followed, peeling the plastic wrapper back from the syringe.

"Eva," he said, "this is so unnecessary."

"Not to me." She pulled up her sleeve and presented the inside of her elbow to him, clenching and unclenching her hand until the vein stood out dark against her pale skin. He bent over her, and when the needle entered her arm she sighed with relief and let her head fall back, her eyes closed.

"My poor Eva," he said as he watched the blood filling the plastic tube. "My poor mad girl."

After the lovemaking, which she endured, she fell asleep. When she woke, the man was gone. She got up and bathed leisurely, taking care to wash the mark on her arm. Then she dressed and looked at herself in the mirror. Next year, she thought, I'll be forty. She leaned forward, examining the lines around her eyes and mouth. She had a premonition that the end was near.

Eva dressed and went out into the street. She wanted to eat but couldn't face sitting alone in a restaurant. She walked along the sidewalk, her eyes badly focused on the people who passed her. She would walk until something stopped her.

She had gone sixteen blocks when she heard the music. It was sweet and distant, inviting enough to make her stop and look for its source. She was standing on the edge of a manicured lawn that rolled up to a church. The doors were open; a man stood with his back to the street, his hands clasped behind him, and past him the music flowed out into the cool air. Eva consulted the black plastic writing in the glass case on the lawn which told her that an oratorio concert was under way and that there was no fee, though donations would be gratefully received. She turned up the walk, climbed the wide steps, and passed the man, who only nodded to her, as if to tell her she had made a good decision. The church was crowded, but she found a seat quickly enough on the side aisle, halfway up to the altar. She did all this without thinking, enchanted by the music, which swelled and poured over her. There was a large choir and several musicians scattered across the altar. They didn't seem to be aware of the power of their activity; indeed their expressions were abstracted, like people engaged in mundane work. Eva sat forward, her back very straight, watching them. The music was so rich, so melancholy, it made her weak. She thought of the man she had just left and clenched her teeth. No more, she told herself, no more.

"Eva." Lawrence had said her name once, softly, without particular emphasis or surprise, and then the car had swerved from the road.

How could this music continue without breaking the hearts of all who heard it? What had it cost its composer? Eva looked around her and saw that the audience listened with varied attention; some people were even talking. Her eyes settled on a man a few rows ahead. His coat was very worn, his hair was long and unkempt, a full beard hid his features. He was turned slightly in his seat, his forehead resting on his hand, his eyes closed.

Eva closed her eyes. She saw the white bowl of the sink streaked with red. She opened her eyes.

Once, through her negligence, one of Lawrence's birds had died. She had found him on the windowsill, stiff, his wings outspread. She had tried to close the wings but could not, for fear of breaking the fine, airy bones. She remembered how she had held the dead creature in her cupped hands, seeing for the first time the beautiful configuration of mottled feathers on the undersides of the wings, and she had been struck by the conviction that the force that had animated this cold body must still be somewhere about, still in the room. She looked around herself confusedly, as if she might see it. Lawrence had found her, an hour later, sitting quietly in a chair with the dead bird in her lap, his wings partly covered by a fold of her skirt. He had said nothing and they had gone out to bury the bird in the yard.

The music swept her past this recollection. It was more intense, more sonorous, building to a pitch she knew she would not be able to bear. She looked frantically at her hands, folded but unfolding, in her lap. At last she saw her husband's face; now in the rising flood of music, she heard his voice.

Instinctively she knew she had risen to her feet, but, powerless to stop herself, was driven into the aisle, where she fell to her knees, her thoughts transported, her heart uplifted, oblivious of the cold and curious eyes that fled every corner of the room to settle on her kneeling, now her prostrate form.

Death Goes to a Party

ATALA BELIEVED she possessed magical powers. She was not sure how to use them, or even the extent to which they might be used, but she was certain that the seat of these powers was her eyes and that she could penetrate the deepest mysteries of the human heart with a glance. The question was what to do with what she saw.

She was so vain of her skill that she thought she must be careful not to take advantage of it. When she spoke to people, she usually kept her eyes lowered, for she didn't like the way strangers were drawn to her by what she knew about them. When she did engage another's eyes, it was with intention, and she tried, as much as she could, to behave responsibly and sympathetically in the face of the shocking confessions that were so often called forth by the irresistible penetration of her powerful eyebeams.

Tonight, she assured herself as she fitted the mask over her face and pinned back her long hair, she could be as free of scruples as she pleased. This was, in fact, the purpose of the masquerade, or so it seemed to her. The freedom of disguise was twofold in that it hid one's true identity beneath a mask, while the very choice of costume told more about this dark truth than might otherwise be possible, and told it all at once to perfect strangers. The opportunity to mask gave Atala an exhilarating sense of freedom. For one evening she could look into the people around her with unrestrained avidity, and the partygoers, all unsuspicious, would show themselves to her, secure in the illusion one picks up at parties that no one is really looking at anyone else.

She pulled the black hood over her head and confronted the reflection of her disguise. The mask was frightening, a death's head swathed in black velvet, and the eyes, which were her own keen knives, were surrounded by twin black circles and could not be made out. She smiled at her reflection, but the skeleton's stern mouth did not smile. The mask was hot; it clung tightly to her face, and her breath steamed the inside of it so that it was perpetually damp. But the impression she made would be worth the discomfort. Perhaps she had a moment of doubt, for it must be a malicious vanity that claims for itself the image of death, but she shrugged off her misgivings at once, backing away from the mirror to take in a longer view of her costume. The effect was startling. No one would recognize her, yet no one would fail to recognize her. She was that dreadful figure we have all seen in pictures, in our dreams, in brooding visions, in moments of danger, the atavistic memory we all share from birth, that last somber and cryptic figure who beckons us into the dark valley of death.

When she arrived at the party, the host, dressed in his gorilla suit, stepped back without a word to let her pass. Immediately she climbed the long staircase to the back balcony so that she could look down on the people in the patio below. Her fellow maskers, confronted with her ghoulish, eyeless face, cleared the way quickly. As each one turned to look at her, she allowed her eyes to stab deeply, taking in sharp, accurate impressions: curiosity, distaste, fear, outrage, hatred. Once on the balcony she found herself alone, though the narrow space was crowded with people who had arranged not to stand near her. She stood quietly to one side and looked down on the crowd below.

At first no one saw her; then, now and again (she watched the consciousness of her presence move about the patio like an insect) some masker would look up and see her. As each one did this, Atala was quick to meet that person's gaze with deep shafts of light, right into the soul if she could get there. Soon all the maskers had looked at her, though none knew if any other knew that death stood above looking down upon them all. Then, quite naturally, for a long time no one looked at her and she grew bored.

She looked at the rail between her hands. The wood had been painted white first, but now it was blue. It had chipped in two places near her index finger, the first revealing the white coat, the second the wood itself, which was cypress. Atala had a sudden image of the great cypress trees that stand in the rivers just north of Lake Pontchartrain. With this picture still before her eyes, she turned from the railing, unaware for a moment that someone was looking at her. She forgot too that she was disguised, and her eyes, casting only to find the answer to the question of whether there was enough room to pass between a midget and a nun, engaged his. One hears of looks that are like lightning bolts, but that image conjures up something hot that all goes one way. What Atala experienced was like a flash of light, but it was cold and sharp. Her own unwary and potentially destructive eye-beams were engaged by that light, drawn all the way out, then all the way in. She could see it all and it could see all of her, or so she thought. She recognized everything she saw: the searching, anxious soul, the cynical, practical ego, the deep sense of irony, the persistent curiosity to know, the fear of being known, the inveterate will for power. All the qualities she knew she showed forth in herself, if only her "self" could be seen, were there before her in the terrible eyes of the man, if he was a man, who watched her from across the room.

He looked away, and Atala, feeling as if she had been taken up to a great height only to be dropped, slumped against the railing. She remembered herself, her disguise, her powers, and summoned a little courage to take a closer look at what she knew, in this night, she wanted most of all.

His costume was only a headpiece. From the neck down he was a man. His torso was bare, tan and muscular; one could see at a glance that he had chosen to go shirtless out of vanity. He wore a pair of black shorts and old blue sneakers; that was all the trouble he'd taken with clothes. But the headpiece was so stunning and so realistic in every detail that the nonchalance of the rest of his costume only set it off to better advantage.

His head was a wolf's head that seemed to grow out of his shoulders as easily as if nature herself had designed it. The eyes were the startling yellow, slit-iris eyes of a wolf, so cold and unearthly that Atala felt a shiver pass over her, as if an icy hand had grasped her spine. Somehow, she thought, he had fixed his own eyes, probably with special contact lenses, so that he could look directly out of his false head without an annoying little space between the inside and the outside. The fur, she concluded, was laid flat up against his face about the eyes, and the long muzzle built out from that.

He was standing near a bookcase, apparently exchanging pleasantries with the host, who was, as usual, smothering and nearly inaudible inside his gorilla suit. The difference in the wolf-man's method of speaking was remarkable. His mouth moved naturally and the words seemed to flow out of his throat without obstruction. Somehow, she observed, the mouth of the real man had been combined with the mouth of the mask. The teeth were a carnivore's, sharp and white, and the roof of the mouth was an inhuman red, but the tongue gave him away, for it was an ordinary human tongue, too thick to lap up water or to sweat, as lupine tongues do. After a few moments he turned from the gorilla and made his way across the room to Atala. She watched him; she had no doubt that his intention was to join her, and she drew herself up as if she were preparing for a contest. The first exchanges at parties are important and Atala knew they might contain impressions that would be held up as promises, made and broken, in the weeks to come. Though the wolf-man was larger than most of the guests, he moved easily and gracefully through the crowd. In a moment he was at her side.

"So you think you are death," he said, leaning over her so that she looked up at his sharp canine teeth. "But I think death looks more as I look. Why do you imagine life can be taken by something already dead, when it is clearly only life that can take life. Don't you agree?" His voice was deep, breathy, and seemed to come from far away. It was almost a whisper, yet each word was clear. The effect was threatening, and Atala, determined to make the right response, took a step backward and concentrated on looking at a point just behind his eyes. It was a trick she knew for disarming a potential aggressor, but the wolf-man only looked back at her, his jaws open in what could have been a smile.

"You are the first who has had the nerve to speak to me this evening," she said, "so I assume that the others are put off because they think I am a threat. For my own part, I came out only as one who wants to look on the living but may not join them. That is the lot of the dead, I imagine, and as it will be my own sooner or later, I meant to try it out."

"You're a cool liar," he responded at once, and Atala, for the first time in her experience, could not hold the eyes of an interlocutor. She looked down as if she were ashamed. "But your answer is a good one and may be truer than you know."

"In what way?" she asked.

He bent over her so that the heat of his breath filled her ear. "Stay with me this evening, Atala," he said, "and find out what it means to play at death."

Of course, she thought, he could have gotten her name from the host. It did not occur to her, as it should have, that her disguise was such a thorough one the host must not have penetrated it. This slip in her reasoning proved how utterly her costume had failed her. It was a failure that would cost her dearly.

Atala took the wolf-man's arm. They crossed the crowded room and descended the long staircase to the living room, where the revelers were dancing. The sound of champagne corks popping in the kitchen was greeted by shouts of approval. Soon black men with cats' ears, whiskers, and long black tails issued into the crowd, carrying silver trays laden with glasses. The dancers paused to refresh themselves, toasting one another and the big clock on the mantel, for it was nearly midnight, the hour of unmasking. When a tray appeared before the wolf-man and Atala, they took their glasses and touched them together briefly, their eyes meeting in a look of such complicity that anyone would have mistaken them for lovers. Atala had to open the grim mouth of her mask with her little finger to press the wine glass against her real mouth. The wolf-man poured the contents of his glass down his red throat and turned to take another. Atala wondered how difficult it would be for him to remove a mask that seemed so intricately attached to his real face. Her own, she thought, could be abandoned in one motion, and she smiled at the expression she anticipated in his eyes, for the face beneath the death's head was one that she knew must give him pleasure. He handed her another glass and moved close to her to speak into her ear, for the crowd was loud in its enthusiasm for the end of the masquerade. His strange, breathy voice assailed her ears, the words so distinct that it was as if everyone else had fallen silent. "You and I should not unmask until we are alone together."

Atala nodded. "My house isn't very far," she said. "We can walk from here."

"Wait for me outside," he replied, then disappeared into the crowd. She saw him again at the kitchen door, where he held up a bottle and two glasses over the crowd, indicating his intention to go out the back and circle the house to the front.

Now Atala had another moment in which to consider the possibilities of her folly, but she paused only to finish the glass of wine in her hand. Then she began to make her way through the crowd of revelers. It was to be a night of unexpected meetings, unprecedented flirtations. The host had taken off the head of his gorilla suit and was waltzing ponderously around the room with a pale-faced young man dressed as a rabbit. On the back balcony a witch stretched up on her toes to kiss a pumpkin. And Atala, gazing through the eye holes of her death mask, paused in the doorway before going out to the wolf-man, who stood on the sidewalk beckoning to her.

They walked along, drinking champagne and holding hands like ordinary lovers. When they came to her house she produced the key from the pocket of her cloak and turned to him. "I'll be glad to get out of this costume," she said. "It's so hot."

The wolf-man said nothing and she led him up the stairs to her apartment. When she switched on the light he flinched, then switched it off behind her. "If you don't mind," he said. "Light hurts my eyes."

Atala stood near the couch, removing her cloak. Beneath it she wore a black velvet dress, low in the bodice and tight at the waist. She was so absorbed in her own appearance, envisioning how her white throat must look against the black material and how her long dark hair, which she unpinned hurriedly, tumbled over her shoulders, that she failed to notice the change in the wolf-man's expression. At the sight of her pale shoulders his dark nostrils inflated and his teeth were momentarily bared. When she turned to him he wore again his amused look, as amiable as he could be with his queer yellow eyes, and he spoke to her gently. "No," he said as she reached up to lift the mask that covered her face. "Wait." Atala let her hand drop and stood quietly, though she was intensely excited, waiting for his command. He came to her and held her by her shoulders so tightly that it hurt her, though she did not let him know.

"Faces last," he said. Then he lifted her in his arms and carried her through the house to her bedroom. He seemed to know the house, Atala thought; he seemed to know everything. He set her down on the edge of the bed and began unbuttoning the front of her dress. In the dresser mirror she could see their strange reflection, a lovely woman with the face of death, a powerful man with the head of a wolf. The champagne had relaxed her to the point of giddiness, and she laughed a little at the intent look on the wolf-man's face as he pulled her dress down and away. For the first time she touched his long muzzle and found it remarkably like a dog's, hard and unexpectedly warm. She let her hand glide along his face to his ears, caressing him as she spoke softly. "Is it hard to get this off?" she asked. "Is it all in one piece?"

But he said nothing, so she let her hand wander down over his shoulders, down to his waist, where she slipped a mischievous finger beneath the waistband of his shorts. He had pulled his shoes off and he assisted her in pulling away the shorts so that he was revealed to her, from the neck down at least, as entirely a man.

Atala sat up a little to slip out of her underpants and then they confronted one another, naked but for their faces.

"Let me see your real face now," he said, "and then you shall see mine." She sat very still as he lifted the mask from her face, and she sighed with a combination of anticipation and relief that, she imagined, must make her the more desirable.

The wolf-man touched her face gently, then, holding her tenderly at the nape of the neck, lowered his head so that she could reach the back of his neck. "Now," he said. "Your turn."

She could feel his warm breath at her breasts as she reached up to peel away the mask. He made, she thought, a peculiar, guttural sound, a sound she found disturbing and unpleasant.

She felt anxiously about the bottom of the mask for the place where she might pull it away, but her fingers found no fissure, no line of any kind that could be pried apart. What her fingertips told her, she could not at first credit. The rough hair that covered the wolf-man's head grew straight out of the skin on his neck. She felt around the sides, anxiously, then frantically, all the while aware of the heated breathing at her breasts, the peculiar threatening sounds from the creature's throat, and the steadily increasing pressure of his hand at the back of her neck. "I can't find it," she said weakly. "I can't do it."

Then he lifted his face over hers and she saw that what she sought could not be found. His teeth were bared and he salivated so heavily that his mouth was frothy. His eyes were terrible — cold, uncanny, and mad with a kind of lust Atala had never seen before. When he spoke, it was not with a human voice. "Now, Atala," he said, "are we both unmasked."

Then all her silly wiles, all her delusions of feminine intuition, all her strategies, her powers of observation, all the frivolous superstition on which she had relied in the past were nothing to her, and she was stripped to the bone by what she understood to be her predicament. A thin line of terror split her consciousness open like a melon, and she lay in the clutches of the wolf-man as defenseless as a rabbit in the talons of an eagle. Yet like the rabbit, who, as the sweet safe earth falls away, must know there is no hope for him, Atala could not give up without a feeble struggle. The wolf-man smiled to see it as he held her down. His fingers closed around her throat, tighter and tighter, until she could not even gasp for air. A relentless lethargy swarmed over her limbs, until the hands she battled him with were limp. The veins in her face were so filled with blood that she could feel her lips swelling, and the vision of the snarling wolf-man was hemmed in by a solid curtain of red. Through her terror, Atala could hear him, for he had not stopped talking in that breathless, other-worldly voice that came from some dark primordial cave where, perhaps, men knew it for what it was. "So you want to know death," he was saying. "Can you see it? You're almost there, Atala. Can you see it? Can you see it?"

Just as she was losing consciousness, he released her and, winding his hand through her hair, pulled her head back so that her throat was exposed to his teeth. Atala came struggling through the darkness that overpowered her to find herself caught in a lover's embrace, her body entwined with his in such an intimate fashion that she found herself straining toward the man even as she struggled against the beast. She moaned, she gave up every illusion she possessed, and, thinking only that if she must die she would see it coming, she reached up to the ravening jaws and turned his face so that she could look into his eyes.

He drew back. He hissed as if he were a snake; his hand caught her up by the throat, and as the darkness closed in for the last time, she was overcome with sadness and she struggled no more.

Atala awoke to find herself in her bed. The morning sunlight poured through the windows of her room. She was alone. Her costume lay folded on the dresser, the mask of death face down atop the dress. It was, she thought, just as she had set it out before the party.

Her throat ached, but when she got up to examine it in the mirror she found no marks on the fair skin. She walked through the house, sat naked on the couch, and considered the events of the night before. The unromantic light of day so altered the face of her memories that at last she concluded she had only had a run-in with a madman. And who was he? She determined to find out.

Atala put on her robe, made a cup of tea, and phoned her host of the evening before. The party, he told her, had gone on well into the morning and at the end of it a pyromaniac dressed as a bear had set his gorilla suit on fire. Atala listened patiently to his exclamations, then asked the question that preoccupied her: Who was the wolf-man?

But her host maintained that he had not seen this remarkable guest. There was a goat-man, he recalled, a wonderful goat-man who had been found, toward dawn, asleep in the lap of one of those dreadful midget brothers, who hadn't bothered to mask at all. Atala described the wolf-man again. Didn't he remember talking to him near the bookcase; hadn't he seen her go down the stairs on his arm? But her host only complained, "Oh, I don't remember. I don't think I saw him. Do you have any idea how hard it is to see out of that gorilla?"

After she hung up the phone, Atala sat on the floor looking at the carpet. She could hear the wolf-man's voice, she could feel his hands around her throat, she could see again the merciless fury in his eyes. Where was he now? When would he be back? Had she seen a man in a disguise, or was he what he seemed, some creature damned by nature and by fate? Or was it possible that Atala had fallen asleep and only dreamed a wild dream of a meeting with death?

Be it so if you will, but alas! it was a dream of evil omen for Atala. Never would she rest in the arms of any man without hearing the wolf-man's strange voice at her ear.

Never would she close her eyes in sleep without finding him there. And in her waking hours he was always lurking, waiting behind every door, down every corridor, in the eyes of strangers, and when she consulted her reflection, deep in her own eyes she would always find his death-cold eyes looking back at her.

Spats

THE DOGS are scratching at the kitchen door. How long, Lydia thinks, has she been lost in the thought of her rival dead? She passes her hand over her eyes, an unconscious effort to push the hot red edge off everything she sees, and goes to the door to let them in.

When Ivan confessed that he was in love with another woman, Lydia thought she could ride it out. She told him what she had so often told him in the turbulent course of their marriage, that he was a fool, that he would be sorry. Even as she watched his friends loading his possessions into the truck, even when she stood alone in the silent half-empty house contemplating a pale patch on the wall where one of his pictures had been, even then she didn't believe he was gone. Now she has only one hope to hold on to: he has left the dogs with her and this must mean he will be coming back.

When she opens the door Gretta hangs back, as she always does, but Spats pushes his way in as soon as she has turned the knob, knocking the door back against her shins and barreling past her, his heavy tail slapping the wood repeatedly.

No sooner is he inside than he turns to block the door so that Gretta can't get past him. He lowers his big head and nips at her forelegs; it's play, it's all in fun, but Gretta only edges past him, pressing close to Lydia, who pushes at the bigger dog with her foot. "Spats," she says, "leave her alone." Spats backs away, but he is only waiting until she is gone; then he will try again. Lydia is struck with the inevitability of this scene. It happens every day, several times a day, and it is always the same. The dogs gambol into the kitchen, knocking against the table legs, turning about in ever-narrowing circles, until they throw themselves down a few feet apart and settle for their naps. Gretta always sleeps curled tightly in a semicircle, her only defense against attacks from her mate, who sleeps on his side, his long legs extended, his neck stretched out, the open, deep sleep of the innocent or the oppressor.

Lydia stands at the door looking back at the dogs. Sometimes Ivan got right down on the floor with Spats, lay beside him holding his big black head against his chest and talking to him. "Did you have a good time at the park today?" he'd croon. "Did you swim? Are you really tired now? Are you happy?" This memory causes Lydia's upper lip to pull back from her teeth. How often had she wanted to kick him right in his handsome face when he did that, crooning over the dog as if it were his child or his mistress. What about me? she thought. What about my day? But she never said that; instead she turned away, biting back her anger and confusion, for she couldn't admit that she was jealous of a dog.

Spats is asleep immediately, his jaws slack and his tongue lolling out over his black lips. As Lydia looks at him she has an unexpected thought: she could kill him. It is certainly in her power. No one would do anything about it, and it would hurt Ivan as nothing else could. She could poison him, or shoot him, or she could take him to a vet and say he was vicious and have him put away.

She lights a match against the grout in the counter top and turns the stove burner on. It is too cold, and she is so numb with the loss of her husband that she watches the flame wearily, hopelessly; it can do so little for her. She could plunge her hand into it and burn it, or she could stand close to it and still be cold. Then she puts the kettle over the flame and turns away.

She had argued with Ivan about everything for years, so often and so intensely that it seemed natural to her. She held him responsible for the hot flush that rose to her cheeks, the bitter taste that flooded her mouth at the very thought of him. She believed that she was ill; sometimes she believed her life was nearly over and she hated Ivan for this too, that he was killing her with these arguments and that he didn't care.

When the water is boiling she fills a cup with coffee and takes it to the table. She sits quietly in the still house; the only sound is the clink of the cup as she sets it back in the saucer. She goes through a cycle of resolutions. The first is a simple one: she will make her husband come back. It is inconceivable that she will fail. They always had these arguments, they even separated a few times, but he always came back and so he always would. He would tire of this other woman in a few weeks and then he would be back. After all, she asked herself, what did this woman have that she didn't have? An education? And what good was that? If Ivan loved this woman for her education, it wasn't really as if he loved her for herself. He loved her for something she had acquired. And Lydia was certain that Ivan had loved *her*, had married her, and must still love her, only for herself, because she was so apparent, so undisguised; there wasn't anything else to love her for.

So this first resolution is a calm one: she will wait for her husband and he will return and she will take him back.

She sets the cup down roughly on the table, for the inevitable question is upon her: How long can she wait? This has been going on for two months, and she is sick of waiting. There must be something she can do. The thought of action stiffens her spine, and her jaw clenches involuntarily. Now comes the terrible vision of her revenge, which never fails to take her so by surprise that she sighs as she lays herself open to it; revenge is her only lover now. She will see a lawyer, sue Ivan for adultery, and get every cent she can out of him, everything, for the rest of his life. But this is unsatisfactory, promising, as it does, nothing better than a long life without him, a life in which he continues to love someone else. She would do better to buy a gun and shoot him. She could call him late at night, when the other woman is asleep, and beg him to come over. He will come; she can scare him into it. And then when he lets himself in with his key she will shoot him in the living room. He left her, she will tell the court. She bought the gun to protect herself because she was alone. How was she to know he would let himself in so late at night? He told her he was never coming back and she had assumed the footsteps in the living room came from the man every lonely woman lies in bed at night listening for, the man who has found out her secret, who knows she is alone, whose mission, which is sanctioned by the male world, is to break the spirit if not the bones of those rebellious women who have the temerity to sleep at night without a man. So she shot him. She wasn't going to ask any questions and live to see him get off in court. How could she have known it was her husband, who had abandoned her?

Yes, yes, that would work. It would be easily accomplished, but wouldn't she only end up as she was now? Better to murder the other woman, who was, after all, the cause of all this intolerable pain. She knew her name, knew where she lived, where she worked. She had called her several times just to hear her voice, her cheerful hello, in which Lydia always heard Ivan's presence, as if he were standing right next to the woman and she had turned away from kissing him to answer the insistent phone. Lydia had heard of a man who killed people for money. She could pay this man, and then the woman would be gone.

The kettle is screaming; she has forgotten to turn off the flame. So she could drink another cup of coffee, then take a bath. But that would take only an hour or so and she has to get through the whole day. The silence in the house is intense, though she knows it is no more quiet than usual. Ivan was never home much in the daytime. What did she do before? It seems to her that that life was another life, one she will never know again, the life in which each day ended with the appearance of her husband. Sometimes, she admitted, she had not been happy to see him, but her certainty that she would see him made the question of whether she was happy or sad a matter of indifference to her. Often she didn't see him until late at night, when he appeared at one of the clubs where she was singing. He took a place in the audience and when she saw him she always sang for him. Then they were both happy. He knew she was admired, and that pleased him, as if she were his reflection and what others saw when they looked at her was more of him. Sometimes he gave her that same affectionate look he gave himself in mirrors, and when he did it made her lightheaded, and she would sing, holding her hands out a little before her, one index finger stretched out as if she were pointing at something, and she would wait until the inevitable line about how it was "you" she loved, wanted, hated, couldn't get free of, couldn't live without, and at that "you" she would make her moving hands be still and with her eyes as well as her hands she would point to her husband in the crowd. Those were the happiest moments they had, though neither of them was really conscious of them, nor did they ever speak of this happiness. When, during the break, they did speak, it was usually to argue about something.

She thinks of this as she stares dully at the dogs, Ivan's dogs. Later she will drive through the cold afternoon light to Larry's cold garage, where they will rehearse. They will have dinner together; Larry and Simon will try to cheer her up, and Kenneth, the drummer, will sit looking on in his usual daze. They will take drugs if anyone has any, cocaine or marijuana, and Simon will drink a six-pack of beer.

Then they will go to the club and she will sing as best she can. She will sing and sing, into the drunken faces of the audience, over the bobbing heads of the frenzied dancers; she will sing like some blinded bird lost in a dark forest trying to find her way out by listening to the echo of her own voice. The truth is that she sings better than she ever has. Everyone tells her so. Her voice is so full of suffering that hearing it would move a stone, though it will not move her husband, because he won't be there. Yet she can't stop looking for him in the audience, as she always has. And as she sings and looks for him she will remember exactly what it was like to find herself in his eyes. That was how she had first seen him, sitting at a table on the edge of the floor, watching her closely. He was carrying on a conversation with a tired-looking woman across from him but he watched Lydia so closely that she could feel his eyes on her. She smiled. She was aware of herself as the surprising creation she really was, a woman who was beautiful to look at and beautiful to hear. She was, at that moment, so self-conscious and so contented that she didn't notice what an oddity he was, a man who was both beautiful and masculine. Her attachment to his appearance, to his gestures, the suddenness of his smile, the coldness of his eyes, came later. At that moment it was herself in his eyes that she loved; as fatal a love match as she would ever know.

The phone rings. She hesitates, then gets up and crosses to the counter. She picks up the receiver and holds it to her ear.

"Hello," Ivan says. "Lydia?"

She says nothing.

"Talk to me!" he exclaims.

"Why should I?"

"Are you all right?"

"No."

"What are you doing?"

"Why are you calling me?"

"About the dogs."

"What about them?"

"Are they OK?"

She sighs. "Yes." Then, patiently, "When are you coming to get them?"

"I can't," he says. "I can't take them. I can't keep them here."

"Why?"

"There's no fenced yard. Vivian's landlord doesn't allow dogs."

At the mention of her rival's name, Lydia feels a sudden rush of blood to her face. "You bastard," she hisses.

"Baby, please," he says, "try to understand."

She slams the receiver down into the cradle. "Bastard," she says again. Her fingers tighten on the edge of the counter until the knuckles are white. He doesn't want the dogs. He doesn't want her. He isn't coming back. "I really can't stand it," she says into the empty kitchen. "I don't think I will be able to stand it."

She is feeding the dogs. They have to eat at either end of the kitchen because Spats will eat Gretta's dinner if he can. Gretta has to be fed first; then Spats is lured away from her bowl with his own. Gretta eats quickly, swallowing one big bite after another, for she knows she has only the time it takes Spats to finish his meal before he will push her away from hers. Tonight Spats is in a bad humor. He growls at Gretta when Lydia sets her bowl down. Gretta hangs her head and backs away. "Spats!" Lydia says. "Leave her alone." She pushes him away with one hand, holding out his bowl before him with the other.

But he growls again, turning his face toward her, and she sees that his teeth are bared and his threat is serious. "Spats," she says firmly, but she backs away. His eyes glaze over with something deep and vicious, and she knows that he no longer hears her. She drops the bowl. The sound of the bowl hitting the linoleum and the sight of his food scattered before him brings Spats back to himself. He falls to eating off the floor. Gretta lifts her head to watch him, then returns to her hurried eating.

Lydia leans against the stove. Her legs are weak and her heart beats absurdly in her ears. In the midst of all this weakness a habitual ambivalence goes hard as stone. Gretta, she thinks, certainly deserves to eat in peace.

She looks down at Spats. Now he is the big, awkward, playful, good fellow again.

"You just killed yourself," Lydia says. Spats looks back at her, his expression friendly, affable. He no longer remembers his fit of bad temper.

Lydia smiles at him. "You just killed yourself and you don't even have the sense to know it," she says.

It is nearly dawn. Lydia lies in her bed alone. She used to sleep on her back when Ivan was with her. Now she sleeps on her side, her legs drawn up to her chest. Or rather, she reminds herself, she lies awake in this position and waits for the sleep that doesn't come.

As far as she is concerned she is still married. Her husband is gone, but marriage, in her view, is not a condition that can be dissolved by external circumstances. She has always believed this; she told Ivan this when she married him, and he agreed or said he agreed. They were bound together for life. He had said he wanted nothing more.

She still believes it. It is all she understands marriage to be. They must cling to each other and let the great night-marish flood of time wash over them as it will; at the end they would be found wherever they were left, washed onto whatever alien shore, dead or alive, still together, their lives entwined as surely as their bodies, inseparably, eternally. How many times in that last year, in the midst of the interminable quarrels that constituted their life together, had she seen pass across his face an expression that filled her with rage, for she saw that he knew she was drowning and he feared she would pull him down with her. So even as she raged at him, she clung to him more tightly, and the lovemaking that followed their arguments was so intense, so filled with her need of him that, she told herself, he must know, wherever she was going, he was going with her.

Now, she confesses to herself, she is drowning. Alone, at night, in the moonless sea of her bed, where she is tossed from nightmare to nightmare so that she wakes gasping for air, throwing her arms out before her, she is drowning alone in the dark and there is nothing to hold on to.

Lydia sits on the floor in the veterinarian's office. Spats lies next to her; his head rests in her lap. He is unconscious but his heart is still beating feebly. Lydia can feel it beneath her palm, which she has pressed against his side. His mouth has gone dry and his dry tongue lolls out to one side. His black lips are slack and there is no sign of the sharp canine teeth that he used to bare so viciously at the slightest provocation. Lydia sits watching his closed eyes and she is afflicted with the horror of what she has done.

He is four years old; she has known him all his life. When Ivan brought him home he was barely weaned and he cried all that first night, a helpless baby whimpering for his lost mother. But he was a sturdy, healthy animal, greedy for life, and he transferred his affections to Ivan and to his food bowl in a matter of days. Before he was half her size he had terrorized Gretta into the role he and Ivan had worked out for her: dog-wife, mother to his children. She would never have a moment's freedom as long as he lived, no sleep that could not be destroyed by his sudden desire for play, no meal that he did not oversee and covet. She was more intelligent than he, and his brutishness wore her down. She became a nervous, quiet animal who would rather be patted than fed, who barricaded herself under desks, behind chairs, wherever she could find a space Spats couldn't occupy at the same time.

Spats was well trained; Ivan saw to that. He always came when he was called and he followed just at his master's heel when they went out for their walks every day. But it ran against his grain; every muscle in his body was tensed for that moment when Ivan would say "Go ahead," and then he would spring forward and run as hard as he could for as long as he was allowed. He was a fine swimmer and loved to fetch sticks thrown into the water.

When he was a year old, his naturally territorial disposition began to show signs of something amiss. He attacked a neighbor who made the mistake of walking into his yard, and bit him twice, on the arm and on the hand. Lydia stood in the doorway screaming at him, and Ivan was there instantly, shouting at Spats and pulling him away from the startled neighbor, who kept muttering that it was his own fault; he shouldn't have come into the yard. Lydia had seen the attack from the start; she had, she realized, seen it coming and not known it. What disturbed her was that Spats had tried to bite the man's face or his throat, and that he had given his victim almost no notice of his intention. One moment he was wagging his tail and barking, she told Ivan; then, with a snarl, he was on the man.

Ivan made excuses for the animal, and Lydia admitted that it was freakish behavior. But in the years that followed, it happened again and again. Lydia had used this evidence against him, had convicted him on the grounds of it; in the last two years he had bitten seven people. Between these attacks he was normal, friendly, playful, and he grew into such a beautiful animal, his big head was so noble, his carriage so powerful and impressive, that people were drawn to him and often stopped to ask about him. He enjoyed everything in his life; he did everything — eating, running, swimming — with such gusto that it was a pleasure to watch him. He was so full of energy, of such inexhaustible force, it was as if he embodied life, and death must stand back a little in awe at the sight of him.

Now Lydia strokes his head, which seems to be getting heavier every moment, and she says his name softly. It's odd, she thinks, that I would like to die but I have to live, and he would like to live but he has to die.

In the last weeks she has wept for herself, for her lost love, for her husband, for her empty life, but the tears that fill her eyes now are for the dying animal she holds in her arms. She is looking straight into the natural beauty that was his life and she sees resting over it, like a relentless cloud of doom, the empty lovelessness that is her own. His big heart has stopped; he is gone.

The Cat in the Attic

WHY, on the eve of his sixtieth birthday, was Mr. William Bucks, owner and president of Bucks' International, rushing down his own staircase on the arm of his employee, Chester Melville? And why was Mrs. Bucks, the entrepreneur's young and beautiful wife, standing above them on the landing, screaming her contempt at the spectacle of her husband and her lover in full retreat? And why, especially why, did Mr. Chester Melville turn to his mistress and, in a voice trembling with rage, cry out, "You killed that cat yourself, Sylvia, as surely as if you had strangled him with your own hands."

This story is difficult to tell; it has so little of what one might call "sensibility" in it. But it is possible to experience a certain morbid sort of epiphany by the prolonged contemplation of the inadequate gestures others make at love, and, in fact, such an epiphany has of late been proved a fit subject for a tale. Chester Melville's failure to love was matched, was eclipsed, was finally rendered inconsequential, by the calculated coldness of the woman he failed to love, though at the moment we first see them here, this observation would have been small comfort to Chester. He understood, at last, that there was something in Sylvia Bucks that no man could love, something not right; I hesitate to say "evil," but perverse, organically amiss. He had felt something for her, nonetheless. Pity, at first, and a devilish curiosity. She had inspired in him a spirit of fierce possession, and he was touched to the heart by the smoothness of her skin and the soft anxious cries she uttered in her search for the orgasm she could never find, no not, she had confided, since the day of her marriage.

Her husband, Mr. William Bucks, or Billy, as his intimates called him, was an unprepossessing man, tall, balding, his large features crowded in the center of his face anxiously, as if they intended to make a break for freedom. He had an eager, friendly, almost doglike manner that made you forget, when you spoke to him, that he was worth a fortune. His software company was one of the quiet superpowers of the computer industry. He had created it himself, by the power of his formidable will. His natural business acumen was extraordinary and no doubt accounted for some of his success, but it was his will that Chester noticed, even in their first interview. Billy Bucks liked Chester on sight and wanted him as an employee. He persuaded him to leave his secure, uninteresting niche at IBM to join in Billy Bucks' personal adventure.

Before Chester attended his first dinner party at the Bucks' home, he made subtle inquiries among his fellow workers as to what he might expect. He was told that the food would be bad, the drinks first-rate and plentiful, that his employer would be gracious, and his wife unpleasant. She was twenty years younger than her husband, and their marriage, which had survived the pitiful storms of only one short year, was not a pleasure to watch. Mr. Bucks, he was told, adored his wife and would neither say nor hear a word against her.

Mrs. Bucks was flamboyantly rude to her husband, and (this last was confided to him by a nervous young man who appeared miserable at finding himself in the possession of such damaging information) she was hopelessly addicted to cocaine.

Chester went to the party with only mild trepidation. He did not expect to have his own fate altered by passing an evening in the same room with Sylvia Bucks. He considered himself invulnerable to attacks of lust, for he had recently recovered from a long love affair in which he had been driven to the limits of his resources by a selfish, obstinate woman who had made him swear more than once that he would not love her. She had destroyed some small desperate part of his natural self-consciousness, so that he thought he deserved a better fate than loving her would ever bring him. There are disasters in love that serve finally to increase one's own self-esteem; this failure was of that order. But Chester was bitter, overconfident, and unaware that his senses were wide open. Mrs. Bucks seemed to look directly into this odd mixture of indifference and vulnerability in the first moment they met. Superficially she was gay, charming; her voice was a little husky. She was, perhaps, too solicitous, but her eyes couldn't keep up the pretense. Like her husband, she was tall; her skin and eyes were as pale as her hair, so that she gave an impression of fading into the very light she seemed to emanate. Chester saw that she was sad, and a glance at his employer, who stood effusing cheerfully at her side, told him why. Though it had been very high, she had had her price, and it was her peculiar tragedy to be, while not sufficiently intelligent to follow the simple and honest dictates of her conscience, not stupid enough to be unaware of the moral implications of her choice. It was not until much later that he understood this and realized that the eloquent and pleading looks she directed at him several

times on that first evening were not, as he thought, intended to
evoke some response, but were meant to express her awareness
of the acute ironies that constituted her situation.

The servants operated as slightly inferior guests in the
Bucks' household and by the time they bothered themselves
to get dinner on the table, the party was too raucous to care.
It was just as well, for the hostess, who had disappeared into
the bedroom at several points and whose teeth were chattering audibly from cocaine, could not decide where everyone
should sit, though she was unshakable in her conviction that
this choice was hers to make. The food, when at last the
guests seated themselves before it, was cold and tasteless.
The chef, Chester observed, specialized in a sauce created
from ground chalk and cheddar cheese that congealed upon
meat and vegetable alike. Mrs. Bucks paddled her fork con-
tentedly in this mess. He watched her closely and observed
that she never actually brought a bite to her lips. When
dinner was over, the party adjourned to the living room for
more alcohol. Mrs. Bucks disappeared again into her bedroom.

Why did Chester follow her?

He didn't actually follow her. The bathroom door was
near her bedroom door, and after he had availed himself of
the former, he found himself pausing outside the latter. How
long did he pause? It was not a very long time, but as it
was unnecessary to pause at all, it was clearly longer than
he should have. After a moment the door opened and Mrs.
Bucks stood facing him.

"Mrs. Bucks," he said.

She sank against the door frame. "You scared me to death,
Mr. Melville."

"I wish you'd call me Chet," he replied.

She looked up at him, but her eyes hardly focused. She

was wearing a strapless top, and from the smooth skin of her shoulders the scent of the perfume she wore rose and overpowered the air. It was a wonder to him that a woman of such wealth would choose such an oppressive scent; it didn't smell expensive. Perhaps it was some unwanted memory of another woman, a woman one would expect to wear too much cheap perfume, that caused Chester to move a little closer. Mrs. Bucks continued her unsuccessful effort to see him. He leaned over her, brought his lips to her shoulder, and left there several soft impressions. She did not resist, or even speak, and for a moment he was terrified that she would push him away, screaming for her husband, his employer. Instead she sighed and said his name, "Mr. Melville," very softly, nor did he correct her again.

"May I call you?" he asked as she turned away from him and took a few wobbly steps toward the dining room. "Yes," she replied, without looking back. "I wish you would."

So, because of a momentary lapse in his usually sound judgment, Chester Melville entered into a clandestine affair with his employer's wife. He knew she would be a difficult woman, and that he would not be able to trust her for a moment. He knew as well that she would never be content with him, for she was committed to her need, not for love, but for some distraction from what must have been a dreadfully empty and insensitive consciousness. But it was partly this insensitivity that attracted Chester, for it made him want to give her a good shaking. He was also, after that first awkward kiss in the hall, mesmerized by her physical presence. She had a feline quality about her, especially in the way she moved, that made him feel as one does when watching a cat, that the cool saunter strings the beast together somehow, that it is the sister to the spring.

Chester was gratified to find that Sylvia had no desire to speak ill of her husband. In fact, she rarely mentioned him. There was, however, someone who competed with Chester for his mistress's affections. Though Sylvia had not been wealthy long, she had adopted the absurd custom many wealthy people have of making a great fuss about small matters. The smaller they were, the more they might appear as vital cogs in the great machine of her life. One of these manias was her cat, Gino, who was a constant consideration in all her plans. It was as if, should she disappear in the next moment, there wouldn't be enough servants left behind to care for his needs or understand his temperament. In her imagination Gino was always longing for her company, always disappointed, even disapproving, when he got it.

One evening, while Billy Bucks was inspecting a new plant in Colorado, Chester Melville sat on an uncomfortable bar stool at the Bucks' establishment, drinking a glass of white wine and talking affably with his cantankerous mistress. Gino appeared suddenly in the doorway, as if to present himself for inspection. Sylvia squealed at the sight of him, pushed roughly past Chester, and scooped the cat up into her arms, repeating his name in a sensuous voice she reserved for him alone. Chester noticed that he was very large for a cat, and that his shoulders had the meatiness of an athlete's. He allowed himself to be squeezed and fussed over, turning his strong body slowly, sinuously, against his mistress's straining, perfumed bosom, but he kept his cold green eyes on Chester.

He seemed to size up the competition. "So you're here too," his eyes informed Chester. He had a wonderful deep frown, as if nothing could be more distasteful than what he contemplated. When he was released and set upon the counter, he walked quickly to Chester and, standing before him, considered his face, feature by feature.

"Oh, he's looking at you," Sylvia cried.

Chester was not moved to respond, and Gino, for his part, did not so much as turn an ear in her direction. After a few moments he strode away, not toward his anxious mistress, who stretched out her arms invitingly, but to the end of the counter, where he stopped, looked over his shoulder, and cast Chester one more penetrating, almost friendly look before he leaped soundlessly to the floor.

"That's an interesting cat you have," Chester observed.

"Oh, Gino," Sylvia replied. "Gino is wonderful. Gino is my love."

Chester was to see Gino many times. Each time he was so impressed with the animal, with his cool manner and athletic beauty, that he found himself looking at other cats only to see how poorly they compared with Gino. But he was to remember him always as he was that last afternoon, a few months after their first encounter, stretched out on Sylvia's bed, one heavy paw resting on a silken negligee, his long tail moving listlessly back and forth across the arm of a sweater. The bed was strewn with Sylvia's clothes; a suitcase lay open, half packed, at the foot; and Sylvia herself stood, half clad, nearby. She was fumbling helplessly with a silver cocaine vial, a gift from her husband, but she could scarcely see it through her tears. Chester stood leaning against the dresser. "It's not going to do you any good to run away if you take two bags of cocaine with you," he was saying. "You need to think things through, you need to be alone, and you need to leave the coke behind."

"I need to get away from you," she said. "Not cocaine."

"Sylvia." He sighed.

The vial gave way and she tapped a thin line of the white powder across her forearm.

"Sylvia," he said again. "I love you."

At this moment Gino stood up and began to stretch his back legs. Sylvia gathered him up. "No one loves me but Gino," she crooned to the indifferent animal. "Gino's going with me. I promised him a yard, I always promised him a yard, and now he'll have one."

The "yard" was, in fact, one thousand acres of Virginia pine forest. Sylvia was running away, but her destination was her husband's summer place, a building designed to house nine or ten male aristocrats intent on a return to nature. It looked rough, but it wasn't. There were servants, a wine cellar, a kitchen created to serve banquets. Here Sylvia proposed to spend a week alone, because, as she told her sympathetic spouse, the chatter and confusion of city life were wearing her down. She told Chester Melville that on her return she would give him the answer to his proposal that she leave her husband. At that moment in the bedroom, she determined to take Gino with her, nor could she be dissuaded from this resolution by any appeal, not about the impracticality of the plan or the unnecessary strain to the animal's health. No, Gino must go, and so he went. He was tranquilized, shoved into a box, and loaded into the airplane with Mrs. Bucks' suitcases. One can only imagine the horrors of the three hours spent in the howling blackness of the airplane, the strange ride along the conveyor belts to his impatient mistress, who pulled him out of the box at once and, cooing and chattering, carried him to the car. When they arrived at the estate, Gino was given an enormous meal, which he could scarcely eat, and then Sylvia carried him to the back terrace, overlooking a wilderness of extraordinary beauty, and set him free. "Here's your yard," she said.

In the week that followed, Gino took advantage of the outdoors, but Sylvia did not. She moved about restlessly from room to room, annoying whomever she encountered. She made a particular enemy of Tom Mann, the caretaker of the estate. Most of the year he lived alone on the property; he had a small cottage a hundred yards from the house, and he exhibited the silent humorlessness that comes of too much solitude. He loved the property and probably knew it better than its owner ever would. Sylvia's unexpected presence was an annoyance to him, and he couldn't disguise his personal distaste for her. She made the great mistake of offering him some cocaine, and the expression on his face as he declined to join her told her clearly what he thought of her.

She was miserable, but she tried to amuse herself. She made desperate late-night phone calls. She forced the cook to prepare elaborate meals she didn't eat. She played rock records loud enough to be heard on the terrace, where she danced by herself, or with Gino in her arms, until she collapsed in tears of frustration. She took three or four baths a day, watched whatever was on television, and tried, without success, to read a book about a woman who, like herself, was torn between her rich husband and her lover. At the end of a week, she had decided only that she must have a change. She packed her bags and inspected Gino's traveling box. An hour before she was to leave, she went to the back door and called her beloved pet.

But he didn't respond. She called and called, and she made the cook call. Then she enlisted Tom Mann in the search, and together they scoured the house and the grounds, but the cat was not to be found. At last she was forced to go without him. He would show up for dinner, they all agreed, and he could be sent on alone the next day. So she went to the airport, anxious but not hysterical. The hysteria started that night, when Tom Mann called to say Gino had not shown up for supper.

Sylvia's first response was to inform Tom Mann that he was

fired, an action that brought down on her, for the first time in their marriage, the clear disapproval of her husband. "The man has worked for me for twenty years," he told her petulantly. "He's completely trustworthy and he can't be replaced."

"He finds Gino, he goes, or I go," she responded. "It's that simple."

But it wasn't that simple. Billy Bucks was forced to call his employee and apologize for his wife's behavior. "She's not herself," he explained, though he had begun to suspect the unhappy truth, which was that Sylvia was, at last, entirely herself. "She's so fond of that cat," he concluded limply. Tom Mann, who knew his own worth, told his employer that he would continue in his post on the condition that he be spared any future communication with Mrs. Bucks. Billy, humiliated and chagrined, agreed.

The staff at the estate was instructed to make the search for Gino their first priority. Two days after Sylvia's departure, the big house was searched, but since Gino was not found and no one was staying in it, Tom Mann closed it up, as was his custom, and retired to his own cottage. He was of the opinion that Gino had taken to the woods, and the only consolation he could offer his employer was the probability that, as the animal had not turned up dead, he might yet be alive.

Sylvia spent the next three weeks in a constant state of panic, and she poured out her bitterness upon the two men who, in her myopic view, were the authors of her woe. Chester Melville knew what Billy Bucks suffered, and though he could not openly sympathize with him, he found himself curiously drawn to his employer. The two men worked closely, like men under fire, bound together by the camaraderie of terror. Every evening Billy called Tom Mann and received his monosyllabic report while his wife stood nearby, her eyes filled with bitter tears, her cocaine vial clenched in her angry fist.

Then Gino was found. Tom Mann was bothered by a leak in his roof, and a cursory inspection revealed that a large section needed to be reshingled. He remembered that there were a number of shingles in the attic of the house, though how they had arrived there he didn't know. He walked hurriedly through the cold empty rooms, hardly looking about him, for there was nothing indoors that he really cared for. Up the stairs he climbed, his heavy steps echoing hollowly in the still, cool air. When he opened the attic door, the sick, sweet smell of death rushed over him, chilling him like a blast of cold air, and he remembered, all at once and clearly, that just three weeks ago he had come up here to store an awning he'd taken down for the winter, that he'd left the door open for a while, and now he knew that Gino, whose emaciated corpse lay before him, the death-frozen jaws coated with the plaster he'd chewed out of the wall in his futile struggle for life, Gino must have come in without his knowledge. Tom Mann was not a man easily moved, but the pitiful condition of the once powerful animal brought a low moan to his lips.

Gino was buried within the hour. The caretaker chose a spot near his own house, at the foot of a weeping willow tree he himself had planted twenty years earlier. He marked the grave with a flat stone to keep the body from being disinterred by passing animals. When this was done he phoned his employer and told him of Gino's fate.

Chester Melville was sitting in Billy Bucks' office when the call came through. He knew the substance of the message at once, simply by observing the sudden pallor of Bucks' complexion and the feebleness with which he concluded the call. "I'll tell Mrs. Bucks at once," he said. "I appreciate your call, Tom." He placed the receiver carefully into its cradle and rubbed his eyes with the heels of his hands.

"Gino's dead," Chester said.

Billy lowered his hands slowly and stared at his employee. He had heard everything in those two words, and he knew, though he had never suspected it for a moment, that he was addressing his wife's lover. The two men looked at each other disconsolately. "I can't tell her over the phone," Billy said at last. "I'll have to go home. Will you come with me?"

"Sure," Chester said, "if you think it will help."

"I think it will help me," Billy replied.

So the two men left the safety of their office building and trudged wearily through the snowy streets to Bucks' palatial flat. Sylvia was drinking coffee and perusing a magazine when they came in, and the sight of their grim faces so unnerved her that she let the magazine slip to the floor.

"Tom Mann called," Billy said. "I'm afraid it's bad news."

The scene that followed went on for a long time. Gino, who had been in reality a hearty, handsome, greedy, and independent beast, who had probably not spent one moment of his intensely feline life longing for anything that might come to him in human form, who had tolerated his mistress as cats do, was now resurrected as the only real love Sylvia had ever known. In the midst of her furious accusations, Chester realized that he had been willing to put his happiness, his job, and his entire future on the line for a woman who, because she knew herself so well, could only scorn any man who was mad enough to love her. He also observed that Billy Bucks knew this as well, but had married her anyway. As the two men beat their retreat down the stairway, Chester, overcome by his sense of his own foolishness, shouted back to her, "You killed that cat yourself, Sylvia, as surely as if you had strangled him with your own hands."

When they were gone, Sylvia smashed her husband's heirloom crystal, but that, she thought, could be replaced. She took a large knife from the kitchen and slashed a small Corot landscape, a particular favorite of her husband's, until it hung from the frame in strips. Then she went to the bedroom and ripped his down pillow until the feathers rose about her like a snowstorm. All she could hear was her lover's parting remark. She began to stab and stab her marriage bed itself, calling out to Gino as she drove the knife deeper and deeper, but nothing she could do would bring poor Gino back to her, nothing she could ever do.

The Freeze

THAT NIGHT, as Anne was dressing in the bathroom, she took a long dreamy look at herself in the mirror. She had finished her make-up. This was the look she always gave herself, critical yet sympathetic; it was intended as a look at the make-up. She was forty years old, twice divorced, a woman who, half a century ago, would have been a statistical failure. But she didn't feel, really, as if she had failed at anything. She looked as good as she ever had. She was strong and healthy and she supported herself and her daughter all alone. She liked being alone, for the most part; she especially liked waking up alone, and she had no intention of changing this, yet she was so pleased by her own reflection in the mirror, it was as if she thought someone else saw her, as if someone were in love with her. And yes, she told herself, pulling the blue silk dress carefully over her head, perhaps someone was in love with her and perhaps she would find out about it tonight.

These were not the vague fancies of middle age. She had a lover in mind and there was a good chance that he would be at this party. But it was absurd, she told herself, joking with herself, because it would have been absurd to anyone else. He was nearly twenty years younger than she. Aaron, she thought, invoking his presence with his name. A rich, charming college student who could certainly find better things to do with his time than make love to a woman twice his age.

She had seen him five times. First, at a friend's, the same friend who was giving this party. He had come in with Jack, the son of the house, a bright, ugly boy who reminded Anne of her high school students. They passed through the kitchen; they were going to play tennis, but Jack paused long enough to introduce his new friend, Aaron Fischer. Anne's first impression of him was indifferent. He was clearly Jewish, his curly hair was blond, his complexion was clear and a little flushed. He looked intelligent. Anne was accustomed to searching for signs of intelligence in the young; it was her profession. He met her eyes as he shook her hand, a firm, self-assured handshake, with a look to match it. She didn't think he really saw her. Jack exchanged a few words with his mother and they went out, but as he turned away from her, Aaron nodded curtly and said, "Peace." They were gone.

"He's an interesting boy," her friend observed.

"I haven't heard anyone say 'Peace' since 1962," Anne replied.

"I hear he has principles too." The two women raised their eyebrows at each other.

"He must be some kind of throwback," Anne concluded.

She saw him again, a week later, as she was coming out of the university library. To her surprise he recognized her. "Anne," he said. "What are you doing here?"

She stammered. She had learned that Yukio Mishima had written a play about the wife of the Marquis de Sade, and, not finding it at the local bookstore, she had come to the library on purpose to read it. It had proved amusing and entirely unshocking, but the title alone was not something she thought this young man would appreciate. "I was just doing a little research," she said. "I'm a teacher, you know."

"You teach here?" He looked surprised, impressed.

"No. I teach at the arts high school."

"Oh," he said, "I've heard of that." Now, she thought, they would part. But he was interested and appeared to have nothing more important to do than stand on the library stairs chatting with a stranger. After a few more exchanges he suggested coffee, which, he said, was what he was out for, and she agreed.

They went to the bright, noisy university cafeteria, had three cups of coffee each, then proceeded to the dark cavernous university tavern, where they shared a pitcher of beer. Aaron talked with such ease and his range of interests was so wide that Anne, who had expected nervous chatter about his classes, found herself completely charmed. He was idealistic, almost militant in his adherence to a code, though precisely what code Anne couldn't make out. He was a political science major, this was his last year, and then he was going to medical school. By the time they parted, when Anne explained that she must pick up her daughter, who was visiting a friend, Aaron had her phone number scribbled in his small leather notebook. He promised to call. The med school applications were voluminous; he had not, in his expensive education, been taught to use a typewriter; and Anne had offered, had insisted on helping him.

Then followed two long evenings in her living room. The applications were more tedious and time-consuming than she had imagined. Aaron exclaimed over the stupidity of the personal questions. Anne moaned every time she saw the printed grid that meant she had to retype his entire undergraduate transcript. The first night, they finished off a bottle of red wine and, when they were done, sat talking comfortably for another hour before Aaron noted the time and hurried off, apologizing for having stayed so late and for having drunk all of her wine.

The next night he arrived with a bottle of champagne. They shared it sparingly as they worked over his applications, and at the end of a few pleasant hours, half of them were ready to be mailed. Aaron was thorough; he was applying to sixty schools.

She was charmed by him, by his youth, by his confidences, by his manner, which was so preternaturally social that she couldn't be sure how much of the pleasure he appeared to take in her company was simply the pleasure he took in any company. He lounged on her couch and looked about her apartment with an appreciative eye, and when he observed that it was time to go (he had a chemistry test at eight in the morning and he hadn't opened a book yet), he added that he did not want to go.

Was he asking to stay?

Anne was cautious. She discussed the matter with her friend, who assured her that it did sound as if the boy was more than superficially interested. And he was a delightful boy; in only a few years he would be, they agreed, a remarkable man. He might be shy; he might fear, as she did, that the attraction he felt for her was something he should not explore. He might think she thought of him as a child and be uncertain or unable to make the first move. Anne might have to make this move, whatever it was, herself. She should be careful. The timing in such matters was extremely delicate; on this the two women were in complete agreement. Anne would see him one more time, to finish the applications, but she might have to wait longer.

Their last meeting was a short one. He had everything completed; it was a matter of a few minutes' typing. He was in a hurry and he complained bitterly of the cause for it. "I have a date," he said. "This ugly girl called me and now I have to go to this stupid party. Why can't I say no? Why didn't I say no?"

"Perhaps she'll be intelligent," Anne suggested.

"No, she won't. She isn't. She's in my eco class and she's failing."

"Do girls call you a lot?" she inquired, pulling the last page out of the typewriter to indicate that the question didn't really interest her.

"Only ugly girls." He gave her a perplexed frown, designed to make her smile.

In a few minutes he was gone.

For two weeks Anne agitated herself with various fantasies. She lay in her bed at night, clutching her pillow, telling herself how it would be, how it would surely be. Their love-making would be dizzying; in fact, the first time would be such a relief for them both that they would collapse into each other's arms with the breathless passion of some long-frustrated, star-crossed Victorians. Then afterward she would laugh and tell him how hard it had been, because of their age difference and because they were so many worlds apart, to admit to herself that she was in love with him. For she was in love, she thought with a growing sense of wonder. Was it possible? She was in love as she had not been since she was a girl, only this was harder to bear and more intense, because she knew exactly what it was she wanted. And it wasn't a home, a family, his money, a ride in his Porsche. She would be content if they never left her apartment and she knew none of his friends. She only wanted him to make love to her; that was all.

And now she stood, dressed, perfumed, made up, before her bathroom mirror, and she assured herself that it would be tonight. He would be there as he had promised her friend, and he would be there just for her. She would look different, so elegant that he would be taken by surprise. The dress was perfect; her dark hair, swept back and up in a fashion he had not seen, gleamed with health and life. He would see at a glance that she was perfect for him.

She stepped into her shoes, threw her reflection a last affectionate look, turned out the overhead light, and went into the hall. Hannah stood in the doorway of her daughter's room. "Anne," she said, "you look so nice. What a beautiful dress."

Anne blushed at the admiration she saw in the girl's eyes. "Do you like it?" she said, turning before her.

"It's lovely," the girl said.

Anne's heart swelled with pleasure. As they walked together to the living room it struck her that she was extraordinarily lucky. She wrote her friend's phone number on the phone pad and promised Hannah that she would call if she went anywhere else.

"Don't worry about it," Hannah replied. "Nell's already asleep."

As she walked to the car Anne looked back and saw Hannah standing on the porch. She was waving with one hand as she pulled the screen in tightly with the other. "Good night," Anne called out impetuously, but the girl didn't hear her. She got into her car, fishing in her purse for the keys.

The party was halfway across town. Anne concentrated on driving and on sitting a little stiffly so that she wouldn't wrinkle her dress. When she arrived her friend greeted her at the door. "He's here," she said. "You look terrific."

"Is he alone?" Anne asked.

"Yes. He's in the back, by the bar. I'll take you there."

"That's a good sign, don't you think?" Anne asked. They passed through the bright rooms filled with glittering crystal, hothouse flowers, silver trays of food, and chatting groups of people. "Your house looks great," she added.

"That he's by the bar?" her friend inquired.

"No, that he's alone," Anne replied.

"Of course it's a good sign." They had come to the last room and as Anne stepped inside she saw Aaron leaning against the far wall. He was talking to an elderly man and he did not see her. "It's a very good sign," her friend agreed. "Get yourself a drink."

Yes, Anne thought. A drink would help. Her knees were decidedly weak. She felt like some wolf waiting for a choice lamb to separate from the fold, and the idea of herself as hungry, as looking hungry to others in the room, struck her with enough force to make her lower her eyes. She told the bartender what she wanted in a voice she scarcely recognized, it was so oily, so sly, the voice of the inveterate predator. When she took the drink he caught her eye and smiled. "This is a party," he said.

"I beg your pardon?" she asked.

"It's a party," he repeated. "You're supposed to be having a good time."

Then she understood him and was annoyed by him. "I just got here," she said, turning away. "Give me a minute."

Aaron was looking at her, had been looking at her, she understood, for some moments, and now he detached himself from the elderly man and made his way toward her. She thought he would say something about her appearance, in which she still had some confidence, and she drew herself up a little to receive a compliment, but when he was near enough to speak, he said, "Christ, that's my chemistry teacher. I didn't expect to find *him* here."

"Did you think he spent his evenings over a hot test tube?" she asked lightly.

He smiled, and his smile was so ingenuous, so charming, that she moved closer to him as if to move into the warm influence of that smile. "I did," he said. "And he might as well, for all he's got to say."

So their conversation began and they continued it for some time. Anne introduced him to some of the people she knew, and several times he went to the bar to refresh their drinks. He seemed content to be near her, to be with her, in fact, and she felt all her nervousness and foreboding melt away. The rooms filled with more and more people, until one had fairly to raise one's voice to be heard. A few couples drifted out onto the patio; it was unseasonably warm and the night air was inviting. Anne and Aaron stood in the doorway, looking out for a few minutes. "Let's go out," Aaron said. "The smoke in here is getting to me."

Anne followed him down the steps of the house and out into the darkness. As she did she watched him and endured such a seizure of desire that her vision clouded. She was not, she realized, drunk; though she could scarcely see, her head was clear. She passed one hand before her eyes and gripped the stair rail tightly with the other, not to steady herself but to hold down a surge of energy. I feel like dynamite, she thought; that was her secret thought behind her hand, and then she looked out. What a sweet thing it was to be alive at that moment, with all the eager force of life throbbing

through her, the sensation of being stunning with the force
of it so that if anyone looked at her they must stop and admire
her beauty, which was only the fleeting surrender of pure
energy that sometimes falls to us, without any effort of our
own.

But no one saw her and the moment passed. The patio was
deep; one side was a high vine-covered wall, along which ran
a ledge. People sat in little groups along the ledge and on
the scattered iron chairs, and they stood about in groups
among the plantains and the palmetto palms, talking, Anne
discovered as she passed among them, about the weather.
The weatherman had predicted a cold front, a drop in temperature of 30 degrees, with rain and wind by midnight. And
here it was, eleven-thirty and 65 degrees. The sky was clear,
black, and fathomless overhead.

She followed Aaron, who didn't look back until he had
reached the far end of the patio. When he turned she came up
to him slowly. "Is this far enough, do you think?" she asked,
teasing.

"No," he said. "But there's a wall here."

She stood near him and they looked back at the house. It
was so brightly lit that it seemed to be ablaze, and the noise
of voices and music poured out the windows and doors like
a liquid. Anne detected a melody she knew. "Oh, I like that
record," she said.

"Who is that?" Aaron listened, then smiled. "Oh, that's
Gato Barbieri. Do you like him?"

"I like that record," she said dreamily, for the music, even
at this distance, was languorous and exotic. "It's pretty roman-
tic though."

She met his eyes but he looked away. He had his hand on
a branch of a crepe myrtle tree and his arm was so raised that

Anne stood in the shadow of it. "I'm going to have to leave soon," he said, shaking the ice in his glass. "As soon as I finish this drink."

"I'm a little tired too," Anne lied.

Then he didn't move, nor did he speak. She stood looking down into her drink. She could feel his eyes on her hair and on her shoulders and she thought that he would touch her, but he didn't. She looked back toward the house, taking in the whole patio of people, none of whom, she saw, was looking in their direction. Say something, she told herself, but she couldn't think of anything. Aaron lifted his drink and sipped it; she heard the clinking sound of the ice, but she didn't look at him. The music was growing more emotional; it exacerbated her desire. She put her drink down at her feet and turned so that she faced the young man, so that she was very close to him, but she didn't meet his eyes because, she thought later, she didn't think it was necessary. Instead she placed her hands lightly on his shoulders and raised up on her toes, for he was several inches taller than she. She had barely touched his lips with her own when he pulled away. "No," he said. "No, thank you."

She dropped back on her heels.

"I'm really flattered," he said. "I really am."

She shook her head, hoping that this moment would pass quickly, that she could shake it away, but time seemed to seep out slowly in all directions like blood from a wound.

"Now I've hurt your feelings," he said.

She looked at the wall past his shoulder, at the bricks between her own feet. She could not look at him, but she moved out of his path. "Please go," she said, and he agreed. Yes, he would go. He apologized again; he had no wish to hurt her feelings; he was really so flattered . . . She cast him a quick look, enough to be sure that he was as uncomfortable as she. "It's all right," she said. "I'm all right. But please leave now."

"Yes," he replied. "I'll go." And he walked away. She didn't watch him cross the patio. She waited for what seemed a long time, without looking at anything or thinking of anything, as if she were stone. Then she was aware of being cold. The temperature had plummeted in a few minutes, and the other people on the patio were moving indoors, looking about, as they went in, at the trees and the empty air, as if they could see the difference they felt. Anne followed them, but no one spoke to her. Inside, her friend caught her by the arm and pulled her into the kitchen. "What happened?" she asked. "Aaron just left in a hurry. Are you meeting him somewhere?"

Anne smiled; she could feel the bitter tension of her own smile. "I made a pass at him and he turned me down."

"He did what?" Her friend was outraged.

"He said, 'No, thank you.' "

"That little prick!"

"I've never made a mistake like this." Anne paused, then added, "I was so sure of myself."

"God, what a jerk. Don't think about it."

Anne was suddenly very tired. "No," she said, "I won't."

"Stay a while," her friend urged. "Stay till everyone is gone. Then we can talk."

"I want to go home," Anne replied. "I want to drink some hot milk and wear my flannel pajamas and socks to bed."

"It's so cold," her friend agreed.

By the time she got to her car the temperature had dropped another five degrees. The wind whipped the tree tops and riffled the foliage. Overhead the sky took on a sheen, as if it had received a coat of wax. Anne was oblivious of everything save her own humiliation, which she did not ponder. Rather, she held it close to her and wrapped her senses around it. It was a trick she knew for postponing tears, a kind of physical brooding that kept the consciousness of pain at bay. She steered the car mindlessly around corners, waited at lights, turned up the long entrance to the expressway. There was hardly any traffic; she could drive as rapidly as she liked; but she only accelerated to forty-five. She looked down upon the quiet, sleepy city as she passed over it, and it seemed to her mysterious, like a sleeping animal, breathing quietly beneath her. This must be what death is like, she thought. Coming into some place alien yet familiar.

That was stupid; that was the way people hoped it would be. But what would it be like? She asked herself this question as personally as she could, speaking to herself, who, after all, would miss her more than anyone. What, she asked, will your death be like?

Death was, perhaps, far away, but at that moment, because of her solitude, it seemed that he drew incautiously near, and she imagined his arms closing about her like a lover's. She shrugged. He was so promiscuous. Who could be flattered by such affection when, sooner or later, he would open his arms to all? Yet, she thought, it must be quite thrilling, really, to know oneself at last held in his cold, hollow eyes. Who else can love as death loves; who craves as death craves?

At home she found Hannah awake, surprised at being relieved so early.

"It's getting ugly out there," Anne told her. "You'd better go while you still can." She stood on the porch and watched the girl safely to her car. Now, she thought. Now, let's see how I am.

She closed the porch door and sat down on the couch, flicking off the lamp and plunging the room into welcome darkness. Tears rose to her eyes, but they didn't overflow. Only her vision was blurred and a pleasant numbness welled up, so that she didn't care even to rub the tears away.

Surely this was not important, she thought. It was not an important event. Not worth considering. He was too young; that was all. She had misread him. It wasn't serious. He was flattered, he had said, and that word pricked her. If only he had not said that.

She covered her face with her hands and moaned. Never had she felt such shame; never had she been so thoroughly humiliated. The clear, distinct, precise memory of the failed kiss developed like a strip of film in her memory — his stiffening and drawing away, her own inability to comprehend it so that she had left her hands on his shoulders for many moments when it should have been clear to her that she should release him. He had so immediately withdrawn his lips from her own that she had found her mouth pressed briefly against the corner of his mouth, then his cheek, then thin air. She had staggered away, she knew now, though she had not known it then, staggered to the tree, which had the courtesy to remain solid and hold her up. There she had remained, devoid of feeling, while he beat his retreat, but now the bitterness came flooding in, and it was so pure and thick that she could scarcely swallow.

Ah, she hated him. He had known all along; he had teased her and smiled at her, confided his sophomoric fears and absurd ambitions to her, laughed at her weak jokes, observed her growing affection for him, encouraged her at every turn, all so that he might say "No, thank you," and leave her standing alone, blinded by the shame of having wanted him.

"Well, I wouldn't have him now," she said aloud, "if he paid me." She laughed; it wasn't true. I suppose, she thought, I should be grateful. This sort of thing was bound to happen. Now it's over and I won't ever make the same mistake again.

But she sat for a while, brooding, resigning herself to having played a major part in a dreary business. She was so tired that even the mild activity of preparing for bed seemed more bother than it was worth. But it would shock her daughter to find her asleep on the couch in her dress, and she would be ashamed of herself, more ashamed than she was already. At last, she roused herself.

The wind lashed the house with the same bitter fury she had quelled in her heart, and it suited her, as she walked through the dark rooms, to hear it rattling the doors and windows, blasting bits of branches and leaves against the glass so that they seemed held there by a magical power. She could see through the bamboo shades in her bedroom, and after changing into pajamas she sat for a few moments watching the big plantain tree straining against the force of the wind, its wide leaves plastered helplessly open along the spines like broken hands. The room was getting colder by the minute. She pulled on her warmest socks and, thrusting her legs under the covers, lay down wearily, feeling, as her cheek touched the pillow, a welcome sensation of relief and release. She threw her arms about her pillow and wept into it, amused through her tears at the comfort it gave her. Then she wept her way into sleep.

The sound woke her gradually. She was aware of it, in a state between sleep and consciousness, before she opened her eyes. It was a repeated sound. Her first thought was that it was coming from the wall.

Clink. Clink, clink.

She reached out and touched the wall, then turned and pressed her ear against it.

Clink. Clink, clink.

It wasn't in the wall.

She looked out into the darkness of her room. She could hear many sounds. It was raining, and she could hear the water rushing along the house gutters, pouring out over the porch where the gutters were weak. The wind was still fierce, and it whistled around the house, tearing at the awning (that was the dull flapping sound) and straining the ropes that held it in place. But above all these sounds there was the other sound, the one she couldn't place.

Clink. Clink, clink.

A metallic sound, metal against wood or concrete.

Yes, she thought, it's on the patio. The sound was irregular, but so continuous that it disturbed her. She got up and looked out the window, but all she could see was the plantain tree and the child's swimming pool, which was overflowing with icy water. The weatherman had predicted a freeze, and she did not doubt him now. In the morning the plantains would be tattered and in a day or two the long leaves would be thoroughly brown.

Clink. Clink, clink.

Perhaps a dog had gotten into the yard. Maybe it was the gate. She went into Nell's room and looked out the window. The gate was bolted; she could see it from that window. The rest of the yard looked cold but empty. There was a small corner, the edge of the concrete slab, that she couldn't see from any window.

Clink. Clink, clink.

She diverted herself by contemplating her sleeping daughter. Nell lay on her back with her arms spread wide. Her long hair was sleep-tousled and her mouth was slightly open. She breathed shallowly. Anne arranged the blanket over her, kissed her cool forehead. My darling, she thought, touched by the sweetness of her daughter's innocent sleep. My beautiful girl.

Clink. Clink, clink, clink.

She might go out and see what it was. But it was so cold, so wet; the wind blew against the back door, and as soon as she opened it she would be soaked.

The sound stopped.

It was nothing. Some trash caught in a bush, blown free now.

She looked at the clock as she went back to bed. It was 3:00 A.M. She curled down under the blankets and pulled her pillow down next to her. It was a bad habit, she thought, clutching this pillow like the mate she didn't have. She thought of Aaron.

Clink. Clink, clink.

It was nothing, she thought. Some trash caught in a bush. She would throw it away in the morning. Now it was important not to think, not about the sound and not about the party, or her foolish infatuation, or the engaging smile of a young man who cared nothing for her. These things didn't bear thinking upon. It didn't matter, she told herself, and she knew why it didn't matter, but somehow, as she lay in the darkness, her consciousness drifting into the less palpable darkness of sleep, she couldn't remember why it didn't matter. Exactly why.

Clink. Clink, clink.

She woke up several times that night. Each time she heard the sound, but she would not listen to it. Later she was to recall that, though it was a small, innocuous sound, there had been in it something so disturbing that she shuddered each time she woke and realized that, whatever it was, it was still going on.

Eventually she woke and it was morning. Her daughter stood next to the bed, looking down at her anxiously.

"It's too early," Anne complained.

"It's cold in my room. Can I get in bed with you?"

Anne pushed back against the wall and motioned the child in under the blankets.

Clink. Clink, clink.

Nell put her arms about her mother's neck. "It's warm in here," she said, curling down gratefully.

"Go to sleep," Anne replied. They fell asleep.

An hour later, when Anne woke and understood that she was awake for the day, she found herself straining to hear the sound. It had stopped. She didn't think of it again, not while she made pancakes for Nell, nor when she browsed leisurely through the morning paper, nor when she stood amidst a week's worth of laundry, sorting the colors and textures for the machine. She collected a pile of clothes in her arms and balanced the soap box on top. Opening the back door to get to the laundry room was always a problem. She worked one hand free beneath the clothes and turned the knob. The door was opened but it had cost her two socks and an undershirt, which lay in the doorway at her feet. Bending down to get them would only mean losing more. Leaving the door open would let the heat out. She bent her knees, reaching down without bending over, like an airline stewardess in bad weather. She retrieved the strayed garments, but the soap powder took the opportunity to fall open, and a thin stream of white fell where the socks had been. "Shit," she said, stepping out onto the patio. In that moment she saw the dead cat.

His body lay in the corner of the patio. In her first glance she knew so much about him, so much about his death, that she closed her eyes as if she could close out what she knew. He lay on his side, his legs stretched out unnaturally. His fur was wet and covered with bits of leaves and dirt. She couldn't see his face, for it was hidden by a tin can, a one-pound salmon can. Anne remembered having thrown it away a few days earlier. The can completely covered the animal's face, up to his ears, and even from a distance she could see that it was wedged on tightly.

"Oh, Jesus," she said. "Oh, Christ."

Anne put the laundry in the washing machine and went back to the yard for a close look. She crouched over the dead animal, pulling her sweater in tightly against the cold. He was a large cat; his fur was white with patches of gray and black. Anne recognized him as one of several neighborhood cats. Someone might feed him regularly and might look for him; she had no way of knowing. The can over his face made him look ludicrous. It would have been funny had she not listened for so many hours to his struggles to free himself. If I'd gone out, she thought, I could have pulled it off. Now she had to deal with the corpse.

When she went inside she found Nell stretched out on her bed with her favorite comic books arranged all about her.

"There's a dead cat in the yard," Anne said.

The child looked up. "There is?"

"He got his face stuck in a salmon can."

Nell sat up and strained to look out the window.

"You can't see him from here. He's in the corner. I don't think you want to see him."

"I want to see him," she said, getting out of bed. "Where is he? Come show me."

"Put your robe on, put your slippers on," Anne said. "It's freezing out there."

Nell pulled on her slippers, hurriedly wrapped herself in her robe, and went to the door. Anne followed her disconsolately. They went out and stood side by side, looking down at the dead cat.

"What a way to go," Anne remarked.

Nell was quiet a moment; then she said in a voice filled with pity, "Mama, can't you take that can off his face?"

Anne hesitated. She was not anxious to see the expression such a death might leave on its victim's face. But she understood the justice of the request. She grasped the can, thinking it would fall away easily, but instead she found she had lifted the animal's head and shoulders from the concrete. The stiffness that was communicated to her fingertips shocked her; it was like lifting a board, and she laid the can back down gingerly. "It's stuck," she said. "It won't come off."

They stood quietly a few moments more. "Should we bury him?" Nell asked.

"No. Dogs would come and dig him up."

"What can we do then?"

"I'll call the city. They have a special number. They'll come pick him up."

"The city?" the child said.

"Well, the Sanitation Department."

They went inside. "That's like the garbage men," the child observed. "You're not going to put him in the garbage can?"

"No. I'll put him in a plastic bag."

Nell considered this. "That will be good," she said. "Then some baby won't come along and see him and be upset."

Later Anne called the Sanitation Department. The man she spoke with was courteous. "Just get it to the curb," he said, "and I'll have someone pick it up. But he won't be there till this afternoon." He paused, consulting a schedule, Anne imagined. "He won't be there until after three."

Anne appreciated the man's precision, and, as it was still drizzling, she left the cat where he was until afternoon. Nell would be off visiting her father. Anne wanted to spare her the sight of the impersonal bagging of the creature, though she had noticed with some satisfaction that the child was neither squeamish nor overimaginative when it came to death. She understood it already as in the nature of things.

At noon the rain stopped and the sun appeared, but it was still bitterly cold and windy. Anne drove her daughter to her ex-husband's and stayed to fill in the parts of the dead cat story that the child neglected. It was hard not to make a joke of the absurdity of the accident. Even Nell saw the humor of it when her father observed that the salmon can would be a new object for dread and suicide threats.

"I can't take it anymore," Anne suggested. "I'm going to get the salmon can."

They laughed over it and then she went home. She didn't take off her coat and stopped only in the kitchen to pick up a plastic trash bag. She proceeded directly to the patio. Now when she opened the door there was no shock in the sight. She went straight to the body as if it had beckoned her.

She knelt down beside the cat. The pavement nearby was dry — the sun had taken care of that — but the corpse was outlined by a ring of moisture like a shadow. She slipped the bag over the animal's back feet and carefully, without touching him, pulled it up to his hips. But there it stuck, and she knew that she would have to lift him to get him into the bag.

She had a sensation of repugnance mixed with confidence. It wouldn't be pleasant, but she didn't doubt that she could do it. Five years ago she would have called on a man to do it and stayed in the house until the corpse was gone, but now there was no one to call and, she thought, no need to call anyone, for she could certainly put this dead body in a bag and transfer it to the curb. She was different now and better now. As a young woman she had been in constant fear, but that fear was gone. It was true that her loneliness was hard to bear; it made her foolish and because of it she imagined that rich, idle young men might be in love with her. It was time to face it, she told herself. Her own youth was gone; it was permanently, irretrievably gone. But it was worth that confession to be rid of the fear that had been, for her, the by-product of dependence. She shrugged against the dreariness of this revelation and bent her will to the task before her.

She touched the cat's side, brushing away some bits of wood that were stuck there. Beneath the wet, soft, dead fur was a wall of flesh as hard as stone. This unpromising rigidity was the cruelest of death's jokes on the living. She imagined that rough treatment might snap the corpse in half, like a thin tube of glass. She lifted the back a little and pulled the bag up to the animal's middle. As she did this she became aware of her own voice in the cold air, addressing the dead cat. "Well, my friend," she was saying, "I wish I'd known; I could have saved you this."

He was a pathetic sight, with his stiff, wet limbs, half in a plastic bag, the red and black label with a great surging silver fish across it all that distinguished his head. It was sad, she thought, such a silly, useless death, though he was certainly not the first creature ever to lose his life in an effort to avoid starvation. She touched his hard, cold side at the place where she thought his heart might be; she patted him softly there. "Poor cat," she said. "While I was tossing around in there worrying about my little heartbreak, you were out here with this."

And she thought of the wall of her bedroom and how she

had fretted on one side of it while death stalked on the other side. Tomorrow his prey might be something big; it might be a man or a child. That night it had just been a cat. But he had stalked all the same and waited and watched. It had taken the cat hours to die, with death cold and patient nearby, waiting for what he could claim, man or beast, it was the same to him.

But that was absurd, she thought. The unyielding flesh beneath her hand told her it was not so. The great fluidity, the sinuousness that was in the nature of these animals, had simply gone out of this one. Death had come from the inside and life had gone out. So that's it, she thought. She lifted her hand, held it before her, and gazed down into her own palm. "It comes from the inside," she said.

Anne pushed the bag aside and lifted the dead cat in her arms. She held him in her arms like a dead child and then she laid him in the bag and pulled the sides up over him. She carried him through the yard to the street. Later two men came by in a truck and took the bag away. The cat was gone. It began to rain again and grow colder still. That night, in that city, there was the hardest freeze in fifty years. Pipes burst, houses flooded, and the water pressure was so low that several buildings burned to the ground while the firemen stood about, cursing the empty hoses they held in their cold and helpless hands.

The Parallel World

IMAGINE that a woman is allowed to go away to perfect solitude. She stays in a little house. The grass around it is high and the footpath that leads to it twists and even disappears in places so that no one is tempted to follow it. The woman stays alone in the house; she sleeps alone at night. Her room is alive with mice that come out when it is dark and cavort, amusing themselves at the expense of her sleep. Soon she will be used to them, will sleep without hearing them, or when she does hear them, she will no longer care to notice them. But at first she can't rest, and in the daytime she lies in the grass outside, for the cabin is among the trees and she likes the sun. Down among the grasses, thinking to find sleep, she finds a new world, what she calls the parallel world. It lies between the ground and the tips of the long grasses.

For a time she is aware of the parallel world only at certain moments. Gazing at the small area of ground between her knees brings it sharply into focus. She hears a dull buzzing of insect life, but she cannot determine, sometimes, if the sound comes from inside or outside her own skull. Then she presses her fingers against the thin flesh that covers her forehead, pressing and pressing while the buzzing sound grows louder and more insistent. She can detect a pattern, like a wispy hair net, stretched over the grass before her, and it seems to shimmer in the morning light as if it were touched with water. She senses activity both in the microscopic world, where strange unicellular animals carry on their affairs in deep silence, and in the macroscopic world of planets and stars, whirling in the blackness of space. The earth, she thinks, has begun to brood upon her fate, and some of us are beginning to hear her sad thoughts.

She fails to find any meaningful activity in the level of consciousness she is herself, thanks to centuries of evolution, constrained to inhabit. She cannot know the earth nor can she care for her fellows who are not, it seems, any longer of the earth. An escape into a world of aliens could not result in deeper loneliness than she feels among beings of her own kind. When she lies among the grasses all alone, it is true that she runs the gamut of emotions, from an ecstasy of unnatural intensity to a brooding despair, mixed with fear, which causes her to suspect her own sanity. But none of these emotions is thrust upon her. She is not confronted, when contemplating the parallel world, with her fellow in suffering. In fact it is the absence of anything resembling human emotion that renders this world cause for joy and, paradoxically, despair.

One night, after a week of such solitude, she wakes up thinking of a time when she was in an audience at a poetry reading. The poet was a Nigerian, a man who was thin, charming, and as dark as the polished wood podium on which he had set his white sheaf of verses. He read a poem about a train trip. He was a prince, she knew this; his father had been the equivalent of a king; and he had ridden the train from the deep heart of the jungle, his father's village, to the city where he was to go to school. He described, in his poem, how he stood at the open window, breathing in the still heat of the jungle, when he saw the angry flock of birds, how they surrounded the train as it broke free from the line of dark foliage into the flat plain beyond, how they dipped and dived about the hurtling cars, shouting to the half-civilized travelers, of whom the poet was one, "Come back to the animal kingdom. Come back to the animal kingdom."

She remembers his voice as she comes out of sleep, precisely the sound of it, the slightly foreign, prep school accent of his speech, and she can see again the way he stood, leaning over the podium as if it were the train window, looking aghast at the air beating about his face as he repeats what he heard the birds cry: "Come back to the animal kingdom. Come back to the animal kingdom."

It had touched her, that poem; it was the kind of poem she sat through reading after dull reading in the hope of finding an image that articulated her own keen sense of longing. When the poem was over, she applauded with the rest, careful not to show how his words had touched her, and after that, when she walked out into the clear, cold night air, she had held those words tight to her chest and, warmed by them, walked the two blocks to her car in a state of extraordinary calm.

Now she sits up in bed and she can hear his voice again, so clearly, as if it is in the room with her, as if the mice scurrying in the eaves call out to her, "Come back. Come back to the animal kingdom." She confronts a new possibility. This solitude may in fact bring her into a new and unexpected place, and because she is frightened of this place, she begins to talk to herself. As she exists only inside the life of someone else, her communication with herself is overheard, though

hardly understood, like the continual conversations that pass
in all of us between what we call the heart and the mind,
which we hear but do not credit, mistaking them for daydreams or for idle thoughts.

She asks herself questions. What sorts of worlds can we
contain? How can we avoid wasting precious time before
death? Are we animals, or are we something else?

In the morning, when she finds a milkweed pod, she splits
open the thick green skin and peels it away, exposing a layer
of cross-hatched, spongy material, like a honeycomb. Inside
this layer is another of flat seeds that lie packed together, so
like fish scales, layered evenly from one end to the other.
Then, when these are brushed aside, she finds the silken
threads at the center, which, when exposed, give off an odor
of inviolate purity. This silken interior is always a surprise.
Children gasp to discover it and will hoard the threads or hide
them in special places, as if they were uncommon treasure.
She imagines, as she opens the silken cache to the light, how
it has been long protected inside its many-layered sheath, and
it is, for a moment, as if she has turned her own soul out of
its hard case and found that innocent pure center where pain
is not felt as pain; that white garden where divinity walks and
waits, quietly, patiently.

Her hearing has become acute. The only sounds are the dull
persistent buzz of insect life and the constant rustling of air
among leaves and grasses. Each day she detects new sounds,
minute sounds: a leaf disconnecting from a branch and flutter-
ing downward, the dull roar that comes from the earth when
she presses her ear against it, and always the steady beating of
her own heart, which she hears from the inside of her ears,
like an obsessive thought. To take her mind off the hopelessness of this sound she stretches out in the grass. For the crea-

tures who live there the grasses are as big as trees, and the shifting and twitching of these trees, their perpetual vibration as they follow the sun in its course, make it difficult to find to-day a roadway or even a path that will be there tomorrow. The creatures who live there move about aimlessly in a colorless void of constant danger, and they live their brief lives without being able to think. They are many-eyed. When they see one another they meet in such a multiplicity of di-mensions that they exchange first glances in a hall of mirrors. Every image is repeated and repeated on the eye into infinity. This is one of the many difficulties that plague the spinners.

For there is always the spinning of countless webs, which cannot be heard and hardly seen. The inspection and main-tenance of these millions of sticky threads occupy every instant of the spinners' lives. They live to spin and spin to live, without artistry but without impatience. In the grasses the webs glisten in the morning light at so many different levels that the view from below is a myriad of sparkling mesh-work, like the high carved vaults of Gothic churches. Here and there among the vaulting, wrapped like mummies, some half devoured, hang the corpses of the captured.

This is the sky in the parallel world. The busy citizens who live below it look up from time to time, but they cannot know their nature or their fate. They can scarcely find their way to one another. And because they must die within a day or two of being born, the urge to life is all there is to life. Finding food, mating quickly and often, knowing time as the incidence of seconds, what can they contain but an hysterical, busy, buzzing force to life?

She learns that even in their furious brief lives there is time for fear. She hears their fear before she sees what they fear. The buzzing ceases for one instant and the silence that consumes its place is the sound of terror. She cannot move, though she hears him now, long before she sees him, tearing through the grasses, flattening everything that comes in his path, a snake, as black as the death he leaves behind him, barreling toward her like an express train. He passes within inches of her face. His flat black eye is cunning, his lifted head almost comical as he veers away from her; but she sees in his eyes that his consciousness is deep, his life is long. He can take his time. He may even bask in the sun, as she does, for the pleasure of it. And he is capable of rage, of cold-blooded stinging fury. A moment after he is seen, he is thoroughly gone, and the reconstruction of the parallel world begins.

It takes some time before she can allow insects to crawl upon her without brushing them away. At first she distinguishes between those she will tolerate and those she won't. Crickets, ladybugs, and a small green beetle who resembles a tiny frog are allowed; ants and flies are not. She is also particular about where they are allowed: on her legs, feet, back, and arms, but never on her face or under her clothing. Gradually these distinctions become less important. An ant is allowed the freedom of her leg. She wearies of rejecting a particularly insistent fly. A beetle enters the sleeve of her blouse and she does not bother to refuse him. A mosquito lands on her forearm and she only watches, sun-dazed, amused by the fussy grandmotherly way she chooses her spot, inserts the long proboscis, and relaxes her thin legs so that her body tilts back to allow for maximum intake. She draws in the blood. A single drop will glut her, the woman thinks; why not let her have it. It seems an inoffensive enough violation, not worth slapping.

She remains now motionless for hours. What began as observation has become an occupation, so that she never feels busier than when she is among the grasses. The parallel world makes a havoc of her body. Her skin is burned from the sun and swollen from the accumulated poisons of those insects who come upon her. When it rains, the water collects in the small of her back and she becomes, momentarily, a watering hole for weary travelers. She witnesses the destruction of a monstrous beetle, set upon by a band of murderous ants. Another day there is a battle between two crickets, who fight on even after one has decapitated his opponent so that his head dangles from a fiber, the fierce mandibles still grinding in outrage. When this struggle is over the victor joins the ants in consuming the spoils, unaware of her gaze, which is fixed upon him. She watches but does nothing, and the cricket for a little time is the lord of all he surveys.

She will not interfere, for she has seen that in this world there is no real hope of another world, though there is certainly evidence that it exists. But the inhabitants are blind to it. They will not see it. There is so little time, hardly any rest, so much to do to stay alive for the next moment. Sleep is snatched in minute intervals, too dangerous to enjoy. The inside curve of her knee, which has been so thoroughly explored by an ant only moments ago, might already have appeared as landscape in his dreams. In the mornings, when she lowers her enormous body down into the grasses, whole cities are demolished, but by the time she rises again she has been absorbed into the parallel world. Roads have been built over and around her, tents pitched in her shadow, information has been exchanged about her true dimensions, her remotest provinces.

She is still all day long until the evening surprises her, for there is no standing and gazing at the sunset in the parallel world, nor does night fall upon it; rather, the darkness rises from the warm dirt like a chill through fever. And she rises with the darkness to find the moon afloat over the grasses, sailing in her black sea, which is not like any sea we know but as flat as paper. The blackness surrounds the moon, is before, behind, above, below her, yet she seems to float upon it.

The woman goes in to her bed alone and there she lies, her sensibilities inflamed from the prolonged observation of the insect world in all its fury; the buzzing, stinging center of it is the center of her dreams. She has two dreams. In the first the image of the parallel world is etched upon her face. She accepts this transformation as passively as certain mountainsides have allowed the hewing of enormous and grotesque human faces. But though she cannot object, her whole consciousness is possessed of a fearful protest, and she wakes in a rage. She is awake, she composes herself, then waits for sleep again, and as she waits the blankets are snatched away, drawn down greedily from the end of the bed as if by angry hands, clawed away from her so that she sits up in terror. Oh, this is the unexpected visceral reality that we know in dreams, yet she is certain that it is no dream. She is propelled from the bed, lifted high above it by a force like an engine, steady and relentless; then she is dashed to the floor, face down, so speedily that she hasn't time to raise her hands to protect her face, and when she strikes the floor, though there is no pain, she can hear the bones in her face cracking, and the blood wells thickly over her tongue. But it is not over yet. She is lifted again, hurled downward again, and she tries only to keep from screaming, for nothing else is in her power.

She wakes; her feet are on the floor before she has time to will herself awake. She stumbles to the bathroom, slams her palm against the light switch, and startles herself into a cry of pain, for in the mirror she finds, beneath her eyelids, two wide, cold, black discs where her eyes should be, two insect eyes, many-faceted and terrifying. She turns her head this way and that; her reflection is everywhere, thousands of images and each one an identical horror. Terrible to see and difficult to see out of, these new eyes throb hatefully in her eye sockets like twin hearts. She covers them with her hands and turns away.

Though she is a horror, she is not afraid, for this is her secret: she exists inside another woman, a very ordinary woman with an ordinary face. Both women know that these new eyes, these terrifying eyes, can be seen only by looking long and deeply into the eyes of the outer woman.

And no one would be likely to look in this way at anyone else.

Later, when she wakes in the empty stillness of her room, her first thought is "I'm still alive."

This thought is repeated, not with any sense of wonder or relief, but as a cold observation. The loneliness of being, at last, fully conscious is intolerable, and the thought of it, again and again, is as futile as firing bullets into a wilderness.

Outside, the grasses hum with activity and the cycles of life and death consume one another, closer and closer.

Elegy for Dead Animals

As a child I made no distinction between my own consciousness and that of the animals, and even of certain plants, who happened into my vicinity. The result of this naïveté, if that is what it is properly called, was a friendship with a small female dog who held me so dear that she would have given her life for mine. I returned her affection with my whole passionate child-soul. On the night that she dragged her crippled hindquarters through five rooms in order to breathe her last at my bedside, I woke to find myself in an unexpected and wholly intolerable region of loss and pain.

Mourn for her now, her sharp foxlike eyes and graying muzzle, her delicate white feet and thick blond fur, her patient, gentle nature. Mourn for her and for all the animals known and lost.

For another dog, a collie whose untimely death I know by legend, who died when he cut his baby teeth because his blood would not clot, who was discovered in his favorite resting place on the fireplace tiles, too weak to move, his face and neck already deep in the gathering blood.

When life pours out of us like blood, the space it leaves is filled at once by death.

Remember cats, who are always surprised by death, who have made their reputations by their defiance of laws we identify with imminent death, who are themselves avid death-dealers, with their needle teeth and unsheathed claws, scourges of the realm of living things that fit between their paws.

Mourn for the kitten a neighbor girl dropped over the back staircase, so that his skull cracked audibly on the wide paving stones below, horrifying his little mistress, who had been told that cats always landed on their feet.

And for the cat, celebrated elsewhere, who smothered to death with his face in a salmon can, whose efforts to escape kept me awake all night, though I did not know what I heard, and blamed the insistent sound of metal against stone on the wind, on my imagination, on the laziness of neighbors who might have left trash uncovered, on everything but death.

Death lies in ambush for all who will defy him, and when he springs his aim is sure and his prey is taken before the great black paws leave the ground.

Mourn now for all the birds in their fragile beauty, whose soaring antics have inspired poets to imagine they must have souls to fly away from death.

For a beloved and noble cockatiel, whose cleverness approached wit, who was called "Farmer" for his habit of throwing seed into potted plants and harvesting the greens he had sown, who kept as a thrall the benighted Basil, a nervous albino parakeet. Recall this exceptional bird, who flew to my shoulders when called and gently nibbled ears, eyeglasses, even the lips, of those few humans he cared for, affectionate bird, wry, mischievous, much lamented, and weep for his final flight into the whirling fan blade of death. Remember his perfect unblemished corpse, wings spread wide, already stiff in my daughter's hands. She held him out to me triumphantly, delighted, mistaking his terrible stillness for acquiescence.

And for other birds, known only at the moment of death. For the bird who flew into the car windshield on a dark night highway, who showed himself feather, claw, then nothing but one drop of blood as red and startling as a cry of pain.

For a mallard duck, pecked to death by his own fellows in a public park, whose struggle for life I witnessed as a child. Helpless to defend him, shocked nearly senseless at seeing nature stripped so bare, I understood that death sometimes chooses his prey by placing an identity, like a bit of grit in a clam, in the murderous group consciousness of his own kind.

And for the sparrow, pried by my bungling fingers from the outraged jaws of the neighbor's cat, who rested so quietly in my hands that I thought I had saved him. I congratulated myself, until a sensation of moisture made me turn the creature over and I saw the torn underbelly from which the entrails hung, too bright, too much alive, and though his tiny heart pumped so wildly in his fragile chest that I could see it through the blood-soaked feathers, we both knew he could not live. And I saw death draw his dull veil over one last jet-black look of terror, so that I found myself with death right in my hands, right in my hands, and I was powerless, useless, alone.

Death sets a seal upon the vision that is all we see and have seen, all we are. The eyes of death are empty and that black emptiness is the look death leaves, no matter how wise or innocent his victim may have been, no matter what he was or what he knew.

Mourn even for the miserable rat, caught in an open roach trap, a sticky tray that introduced him gradually to death; his struggles only stuck him faster. The racket dragged me from my sleep and into the kitchen. He heard his doom in my footsteps, and when I pressed the light switch he must have thought the awful flood of light was death himself, for he screamed as I had not thought such animals could scream. His dying hour was torture; trapped by a giant who could tolerate neither his touch nor his continued existence, he pressed himself deeper and deeper into the gluey trap until he could scarcely move his eyes. My dilemma was how to cause his death, certain as I was that our relative positions (his as a rat, mine as a human) could result only in his death, as if it were some law I would be penalized for breaking. Before the shovel blow ended his ordeal, I saw, and clearly, that though rats may not suffer, as I do, depressions, boredom, loneliness, jealous rage, we do share equally our tenacity to life, our terror of death.

All who live know the meaning of death, and yet who would not scruple to wage a war with death, as if we thought we might be the victors?

Mourn now for all those animals who have died at the hands of men, who have seen in the furious progress of our civilization over the earth only the great two-legged stride of death.

Death is not the end of life but the enemy of life. Death can be no friend to any creature who lives. Those who would long for death court the inevitable; let them be objects of scorn to the living.

As a child I conceived the dream of the animal life. In this dream no animals ever die. Nothing dies, yet the seasons change and the planet teems with life. All the animals, lost and unknown, past and future, lift their eyes in the vast stillness of a starry night, deer and lions, snakes and birds, fish, lizards, frogs, even the innumerable insects, all gaze together for a moment at the starry dome, and they hear the earth as it whirls softly in the black stillness of the universe, and for that one moment there is no death on earth, no death possible, not even in dreams.

About the Author

Valerie Martin is the author of three novels, *Set in Motion, Alexandra,* and *A Recent Martyr*. She was born in Sedalia, Missouri, and grew up in New Orleans. At present she is teaching at Mount Holyoke College in South Hadley, Massachusetts.